BP

He'd found his son.

"Anise, I'm sorry to spring this on you. It must be hard for you. But believe me, I'm not here to take anything from you. Or from Jase." He leaned forward in his chair, wanting nothing more at that moment than to reassure her of his intentions. "I came here to be a father to him. A real father. To help him, to love him, to be there for him. Nothing more."

"I hope so, Harrison." She turned her huge brown eyes on him in a way that confirmed his responsibility to her, too. It would be his job to keep her heart safe, to make her life better instead of letting her live in fear of him and what he might do.

"What do we do now? A paternity test?" she asked, swiping under her eyes with her fingers. "I'm not sure I'm ready to tell Jase…"

The tone of her voice suggested she wanted to add the words *until I find out more about you.*

Christina Miller left her nursing job to become a writer and editor so she could read for a living. With two theology degrees, she is a pastor's wife and worship leader. She enjoys exploring museums and hosting Dinner Church in her home. She lives on her family farm with her husband of thirty-three years. Contact Christina through Love Inspired, Facebook.com/christinalinstrotmiller or @clmauthor.

Books by Christina Miller

Love Inspired

Finding His Family
An Orphan's Hope
Embracing His Past

Love Inspired Historical

Counterfeit Courtship
An Inconvenient Marriage

Visit the Author Profile page at LoveInspired.com.

Embracing His Past

Christina Miller

LOVE INSPIRED
INSPIRATIONAL ROMANCE

LOVE INSPIRED®
INSPIRATIONAL ROMANCE

ISBN-13: 978-1-335-58595-0

PLEASE RECYCLE — THIS PRODUCT IS RECYCLABLE

Recycling programs for this product may not exist in your area.

Embracing His Past

Love Inspired
22 Adelaide St. West, 41st Floor
Toronto, Ontario M5H 4E3, Canada
www.LoveInspired.com

Printed in U.S.A.

Draw nigh to God, and he will draw nigh to you.
—*James* 4:8

For the two dogs I loved the most:
Sugar and Tiny Romeo.

Chapter One

Being grounded was one thing. Being grounded in Mayberry was another.

Harrison stepped onto the back porch of his newly rented home and gazed into the blue September morning sky, wishing he was up there. Moving from San Diego to Natchez, Mississippi—tame. Switching from helicopter flight nurse to ER nurse in a hospital the size of a clinic—tamer yet. But if he had to spend the rest of his life working in a hospital too small to have its own helicopter in order to find the son he'd only recently learned existed and form a relationship with him, he'd do it.

Because although he didn't know his son's name, the young man was all the family he had left. And who knew? Even though his son would be grown by now, he might need Harrison too. At least, that's what Harrison had been telling himself for the past three weeks, ever since the letter came from that fast-talking Nashville attorney.

The letter that changed Harrison Mitchell's life forever.

He looked around the fenced-in lawn, then glanced at his watch. With only ten minutes until he needed to leave for his first day of orientation at what must be the world's smallest hospital, he needed to bring in his new dog—immediately.

In his haste, Harrison ignored the steps, jumping off the porch instead and calling the little brown-and-white mixed breed left here by his landlady, who had asked him to take care of the dog for now.

No sign of Tiny.

Surely Harrison hadn't lost his foster dog on their first full day together.

He quick-walked the perimeter of the lawn, calling Tiny's name and checking behind the flower bushes and the trunk of an enormous tree.

Until a cry rang out from the yard next door.

A desperate cry. A cry of pain.

It sounded like the piercing wail of a young child, like the ones he used to hear in the ER in the early days. But that had been a good twenty years ago, and since Harrison had never raised a child—or owned a dog, for that matter—he couldn't be sure.

"Hey, are you okay?" Harrison strode to the white picket fence. "Is anybody there?"

At the sound of his voice, the cries grew louder, more insistent, seeming to come from the neighbor's back porch. He strained to see around the potted palms and white porch posts there.

Clearly no one was around to help the child. Triage protocol would prioritize a child's safety above a dog's. And the child was definitely more important than being a half hour early for work.

He grabbed the top of the fence, jumped and swung himself over.

Harrison ran a full three strides before he saw a blond woman standing barefoot on the porch, younger than him and wearing blue athleisure pants and an oversized white hoodie. Tiny stood beside her, nuzzling a taller, slender white English setter with black spots.

A surge of relief rushed through him, and then he turned his attention to the woman.

But he didn't see a child.

He skidded to a stop.

"I… I was…" Harrison shot his gaze around the porch, but the cries had stopped. "I heard something, and I thought somebody was hurt, and…"

And his overactive need to be everybody's hero had taken over—again. His cheeks and neck heating, he scrubbed his hand over his face, wanting nothing more than to jump back over that fence and disappear. Instead, he took a step forward. "I was looking for Tiny—" he gestured to the animal "—the dog I'm supposed to take care of. Apparently, I'm not starting out too well, since I lost him on our first day together."

She glanced down at the dogs. "Is that his name? I call him Romeo because he came over yesterday afternoon and spent the day with my Sugar girl."

Her dog took off across the lawn, and Tiny amazingly kept up, his much-shorter legs pumping. Harrison resisted the urge to grab him and run from this embarrassing situation. "I guess we'll have to call him Tiny Romeo, since he seems to be as much your dog as mine."

"I think Tiny Romeo sounds just right," she said as both dogs stopped and focused on a little brown bird sitting on a low-hanging branch of Harrison's ancient tree. "Judging from your accent, I'd say you're not a Mississippi native. So you might not know that, here in the South, lots of people have double names. Sometimes dogs do too."

"Tiny Romeo it is, then," he said. "And you guessed right. I'm from San Diego."

"I'm Anise Armstrong," she said, stepping off the porch and extending her hand. "Your landlady, Miss Eugenia, is my son's grandmother-in-law."

"Harrison Mitchell." He took her hand, instantly intrigued by her soft brown eyes that probably warmed even the heart of the charmingly bossy Eugenia Stratton. Last night, he'd found out just how bossy when she'd insisted on renting him this house, instead of the smaller, already-agreed-upon home across town.

He took a closer look at Anise. With a married son, she must be a decade older than he'd thought, closer to his own age.

"I have to say, that was quite a leap you made over the fence." Now those pretty eyes twinkled as she grinned at him and pushed her long, wavy hair behind her ear. "When did you move in?"

"I got to town yesterday morning, met my landlady and moved in last night."

Her gracious manner and that stunning smile had put Harrison instantly at ease. Not to mention her low, melodic voice. On guard around women as always, he held back a bit emotionally, because he had a feeling this pretty lady could make him forget his vow never to date again—if he let her.

And if she was single. Which she probably wasn't.

Besides, all that mattered was finding his son. Or at least finding Annie Barrett Browning, the woman who, according to the Nashville attorney, had adopted Harrison's son and brought him to her Natchez home.

"I can understand why you thought someone was hurt," she said as the dogs trotted back across the yard. "I guess Romeo—Tiny Romeo—came over and made that racket so I would let Sugar out. He does sound a little like a scared or hurt child."

His little dog trotted by, following Sugar toward the porch. Harrison snatched him up and held him close, rubbing him behind the ears, his heart melting a little when Tiny Romeo gazed at him with sweet brown eyes. "I've never had a dog or a child, so I was at a disadvantage." At least, he hadn't had either until now. "But how did he get in your yard?"

"Not like you did."

Anise flashed her beautiful smile again, and Harrison steeled himself against it.

She peered at the fence near the house. "Look, there's a hole at the bottom of one of the boards. I never noticed that before. Not even when I lifted Tiny Romeo back over the fence last night."

He turned in the direction of her gaze. Sure enough, he saw a freshly sawn Tiny Romeo–sized hole.

"Wait—" She pointed at the bush with the huge deep pink blooms on his side of the fence. "Where did that gate come from?"

Gate? He stepped closer and sure enough, there it was, mostly hidden by the giant shrub. No wonder he hadn't seen it earlier.

Now he felt even more foolish for jumping the fence…

"Miss Eugenia," she whispered, comprehension of some kind dawning in her face. "How sneaky, even for her."

His landlady? "What about her? Do you think she had someone put in this gate?" Maybe the quirky elderly lady had. Judging from the spunkiness and determination he'd already seen in her, she could be expected to do just about anything.

But the hole?

"All I know is that I never saw either the gate or the hole before."

Her tone suggested she wanted to change this silly topic. But Harrison had to admit it might have been interesting to try to figure out who would do such a random act.

"I guess she thought you needed a foster dog," Anise said, her tinkling laugh making him smile. She turned her gaze toward his house. "Will your wife be home today? I'd like to meet her."

Harrison hesitated. Back in San Diego, he'd rarely had to reveal his marital status, since Lisa had been gone several years and he pretty much hung out with just his friends who understood he wasn't into dating or even meeting new women. Life was about serving and helping people. It wasn't about frittering away time and being set up with women he had no intention of getting involved with. And meeting somebody one minute and then telling them your wife was dead the next was just plain awkward.

He cleared his throat. "Uh, I'm a widower."

Instead of the fake sympathy look he usually got, Anise's eyes turned soft. "I'm sorry. And I understand how hard that is to tell a stranger."

Ah, she had experienced loss as well.

"I'm alone too," she said, her voice low and sweet, "but I never know whether to say I'm divorced or widowed. My former husband left our family when my boys were small and immediately filed for divorce. Then he passed on a few years ago."

Wow, this lady might have known even more heartache than Harrison had. He drew a deep breath. "I'm sorry you had to go through that."

A hint of a smile crossed her lips. "Me too.

But I have my sons and grandchildren. You said you don't have kids?"

He chose his words carefully. "Unfortunately, my wife was unable to have children."

A comforting wave of understanding swelled between them, until a nearby church bell chimed the quarter hour and broke the connection.

Harrison checked his watch. Seven forty-five. When was the last time he'd left for work this late?

Of course, in a town this size, there was a chance Anise might know who'd adopted the son of a Nashville wannabe singer and a traveling nurse. But as much as he wanted to ask, he needed to leave for work, so he'd hold his questions for another time. Maybe he'd pay a neighborly visit tonight. This time, he'd use the front door. Or the gate.

"Gotta go. First day at the new job, you know." Choosing to use the gate this time, he carried Tiny Romeo into their own yard and headed for the house.

Inside, he made sure Tiny Romeo had food and water, along with the dog toys Harrison bought last night. Then he grabbed his keys, jogged to the detached garage and started his Harley.

Minutes later, after parking in the employee lot and sprinting inside the hospital, Harrison slowed his pace and strode into the conference room for orientation. After an hour of the usual boring training videos with the other new hires, the director of nursing, looking about nine and a half months pregnant, motioned for him to follow her out to the hallway.

"I'm in a bind," Tara Conway said, opening the tablet in her hand. "I know that when I hired you, I promised you a job in the ER. But would you consider working in a different department temporarily?"

He hesitated, wanting to help her out. But even the ER in a hospital this size couldn't hold as much challenge as he was used to, let alone a medical or surgical floor. "Which department?"

Tara handed him the tablet.

There he discovered an image of a giant, dated RV with the words *Adams County Mobile Clinic* painted in red across the span of its white body.

Holding in a groan, he tried to imagine spending his days in the monstrosity that looked as if it'd been around as long as he had. He pictured himself doing nothing more exciting than taking blood pressures and temperatures, conducting eye exams for truck drivers and instructing people to take the entire bottle of antibiotics, even if they felt better.

"I hate to ask this, but would you consider

the mobile rural clinic?" Tara reached for the tablet he held out to her. "I know how valuable you'll eventually be in our ER. But the nurse who agreed to transfer to the mobile clinic had to take FMLA leave so she could care for a terminally ill family member. Adams County has a lot of rural citizens who don't have access to health care, and they need this clinic."

Harrison caught the fleeting anxiety in Tara's eyes.

"This clinic means a lot to me." She laid her hand on her protruding abdomen, lowering her voice. "I had a hard time finding anyone for this position, because of the lack of challenge. If you'll help me out, I promise to get you out of there as quickly as I can."

He puffed out a breath. As she'd said, it wouldn't be permanent. She could find another nurse tomorrow, for all they knew. "Okay. I want to help you, so yeah. I'll do it."

As she gushed her thanks, he was almost afraid she was going to hug him.

"I won't forget this. And the good thing is, you'll have weekends off. The clinic runs Monday through Friday."

Which meant he could attend church every Sunday—a definite plus.

"We've partnered with Jackson Memorial Hospital for this new venture. They recently bought a new van for their rural clinic, so they loaned us their old RV along with fuel, maintenance and other operating costs, including marketing. We provide staffing and office space, along with parking space in the ER bay," she said, starting down the hall and gesturing for him to follow.

"I want to introduce you to the nurse practitioner you'll work with. While the clinic is completely in her hands, the hiring of all hospital nurses is my responsibility. But since it'll be just the two of you working together, I've given her the final say in hiring the clinic nurse. If she approves, you'll start Monday."

"That sounds fine." At least this introduction wouldn't be as awkward as his last one. His pride still ached a little from his ridiculous mistake in the back lawn this morning.

"This is the clinic office," Tara said.

Harrison stood back and let her enter the small room first, then he strode in, continuing to stew about his earlier embarrassment. Anise had thought Tiny Romeo's racket had sounded like an injured child too. Anybody would have—

He stopped. Looked at the blond woman swiveling in her desk chair, her brown eyes wide. "Anise?"

"Harrison?" She had changed into slim black pants and a white flowy shirt and had piled her pretty hair on top of her head in a tousled knot. Which was cute too. "Is anything wrong? The dogs?"

"You know each other?" Tara asked, plopping onto a nearby faux-leather sofa.

An awkward beat passed, charging the room with some unseen current.

"No," Harrison spit out.

"Yes," Anise said at the same time.

Another split-second pause.

"Yes and no." Anise grinned at him as if they had some sort of secret. "We share a dog."

Tara held up her hand. "Wait a minute. Anise, Harrison's a new hire, and I pulled him from ER and brought him in here because he agreed to be the mobile clinic nurse until I can find someone else. But if this is going to be awkward—"

"No," Harrison all but shouted. "It's nothing like that. We just met this morning."

"But you own a dog together."

"So to speak." Judging from that twinkle in Anise's eyes, she was enjoying this.

Fine, but he didn't want to be unjustly slapped with a reputation on his first full day in Natchez. Especially since he was looking for his son. "We're neighbors. My dog sneaked through the fence into Anise's yard."

Why had he said that? Now he sounded as if

he couldn't even take care of a dog. This was getting worse by the minute.

Anise laughed. "It's fine, Tara. We're just neighbors. Harrison, let me look over your résumé, and then I'll give you a call."

He turned his gaze to the window and the clear blue September sky.

Grounded.

Shut up in a decrepit RV instead of getting to know hospital staff who might help him find his son. Of course, he'd meet a lot of people in the clinic, but asking his patients about his son didn't seem professional. And the clinic job was only temporary. Tara would surely find another nurse soon, then Harrison would move to the ER.

But if his son was living in Natchez and wanted a relationship with him, Harrison would gladly stay grounded in this tiny town's mobile clinic for the rest of his life.

Hire Harrison Mitchell as a mobile clinic nurse? What was she thinking?

As Anise scrolled through his résumé later, she found it so packed with education, honors and publication credits that she felt silly inviting him to her rather shabby clinic. For that matter, why had he left San Diego to come to their small hospital?

He'd listed a friend as his emergency contact. Considering the fact that Miss Eugenia had insisted on renting him the house next door to her—and seemingly had added a gate and cut a hole in the fence, Anise had been certain he was single, even before he'd said so. With Miss Eugenia in her life, she always had to stay on her toes.

She paged down his job application to the question-and-answer section:

Question: Why do you want to work at our hospital?

Answer: Because I want to live in your town. I've learned there is something out there I want to find, and I hope to discover it in Natchez.

This man would be bored silly in the mobile clinic. Not to mention the possibility that a man as intense as Harrison might not be the best fit for the elderly population that would make up the majority of her patients. His leap over the fence had proved that.

She smiled, thinking back to the moment she'd looked up and seen a strikingly handsome man sailing over the white pickets, dressed in light brown chinos and a blue shirt to match his eyes. Anise had to admit she'd been impressed. But could he dial back his intensity enough to make a difference in these rural people's lives and health?

Then again, his eyes had filled with concern for Tiny Romeo, which showed he had a soft side. And the way he'd held the little dog gently and rubbed his ears…

But that stirring she'd felt in her heart was merely because she'd already fallen in love with the little left-behind dog and was glad someone else cared for him too. It had nothing to do with the man.

She sighed, tapping her fingers against her jaw. Since the clinic was scheduled to start on Monday—only four days away—she had to decide about Harrison today. If she didn't hire him, she'd have to call the media and the churches hosting the clinics. Then she'd need to make announcements on social media, telling her old neighborhood she'd failed to bring them the health care she'd promised.

Plus she could lose the confidence of her donors and Jackson Memorial Hospital, which loaned her the RV.

Is this Your plan, Lord?

With no clear direction from Him, she glanced at the clock. Since tonight was small-group Bible study night, a horde of church folk would knock on her door at home in exactly an hour, and she still had to set the table and warm the Texas chili she'd made this morning.

Maybe she should wait a little longer, talk with Harrison more.

Anise reached for her phone, opened her text messaging app, and entered the phone number from Harrison's application. She breathed a prayer for wisdom, then started her message.

Harrison, this is Anise. Can you stop by my house tonight to answer another question or two? I'm having a few church friends over, plus my son, Jase, who teaches our Bible study. It would be a great chance for you to eat a hot meal while meeting some Natchezites.

When he texted back, accepting her offer, Anise packed her messenger bag and locked her office door on the way out. Riding home on her red Honda scooter, she realized she'd hesitated to offer Harrison the job because it didn't seem fair to him. He was used to trauma, independence, fast decisions. Her rural mobile clinic would feel like kindergarten to him.

Then again, Anise didn't exactly have nurses lined up at her door, wanting this job. And since the day she'd moved away from Mamaw Vestal's little home and flower farm near the bayou, she'd known beyond doubt that bringing health care to rural Adams County was the Lord's plan for her.

She'd prepared for this work all these years.

A half hour later, just as Anise settled into the little reading nook in her living room and picked up her new inspirational romance novel for a few minutes of quiet before the storm, she heard her son's Mustang pull up. She drew back her lace curtain and peered out as handsome, dark-haired Jase sprinted up the steps, carrying a book. She dropped the oatmeal-colored panel and waited for her son to brighten the room and her life with his presence.

"I figured you wouldn't mind if I came early, since you're always ready ahead of time," he said as he strode through the unlocked black-painted wooden door, leaving it open and letting the refreshing breeze blow through the screen. He sat in the oversized wing chair opposite her and handed her the thick book with a faded, tattered cover.

"Jase, this looks a hundred years old." She checked the title. *Old Time Gospel Songs*. Then she glanced out the window again, hoping to see Jase's wife and daughter. But the driveway and yard were empty, so she set her novel on the walnut table in front of the window, right next to her grandmother's copy of Elizabeth Barrett

Browning's *Sonnets from the Portuguese and Other Poems*. "Where are Erin and Bella?"

"They're staying home tonight. Bella has a sniffle, so I didn't want to take her out, and Erin's moving pretty slow."

Yes, she would be, since she was eight months pregnant with twins.

"Pastor David loaned me this hymnal," he said, standing and pulling out the bench of Anise's cherry baby grand piano. "He wants us to sing an old hymn for Homecoming Sunday. If you're okay with that, I thought we could practice before everybody gets here."

She got up and took her seat at the piano, leafing through the book's fragile pages. "Do you have a song in mind?"

"Sure do. Page forty-five."

Anise caught his grin. "Let me guess. 'Just Over in the Gloryland'?"

"How'd you know?"

She turned to the page and smoothed the old paper. "Only because you asked to sing this song every evening when you were a boy."

"It's a happy song. It always cheered me up."

Oh, Jase. "I remember. Singing together always made things a little easier after your dad left, didn't it?"

The way he laid his hand on her shoulder, giving it the slightest squeeze, and then sat beside her on the bench—it was almost like old times. The worst times, when the pain of Vernon's abandonment made them sing through their tears. The best times, when she and Jase fixed supper in their little shack, which sometimes seemed held together only by their prayers.

And then Abe would come home—her then twelve-year-old man of the house—and give her the few dollars he'd earned after school, mowing, weeding flower beds or anything else he could think of to help make ends meet. At the supper table, the boys had chattered and she'd smiled and tried to keep up the appearance that they would all be okay.

Later, after Abe had taken a bath and she and Jase had washed dishes in the little sink barely big enough to hold their plates, they'd sit together and sing a cappella, having sold their piano to pay some of the bills Vernon had left behind. Sometimes a silly song they'd learned at church camp, back when she and Vernon had the money to send them. Sometimes a popular contemporary Christian song. Sometimes a hymn.

Always "Just Over in the Gloryland."

Anise smiled at him, sitting beside her, all grown up and fulfilling the call of God and building a family of his own. She chose her key, set the songbook on the piano's music rest and used two hymnals to prop open the pages in case she needed to see the lyrics. "Ready?"

Jase counted out a tempo, and Anise hit the keys for the introduction, playing old-time gospel style as a fast, upbeat old song like this deserved.

As always, on the first verse, they sang the melody together. Then at the chorus, Anise improvised vocally with a throaty soprano harmony while Jase carried the melody. On verse two, they switched, with Jase belting out a Nashville-worthy bass harmony line that made her heart swell with pride.

Her fingers flying on the keys, tinkling the treble and walking the bass, Anise lost herself in the music, the lyrics—the message behind the words as that glory land suddenly seemed near and dear. The song ended way too soon, but Anise put everything she had into the tag, finally playing a flashy ending and sustaining the last chord to make it ring through the house as only a grand piano could do.

"Whoa, Mama!" Jase yelled, throwing his arms around her. "That was amazing! When was the last time you played that song?"

"Probably five years ago, at least. But don't be impressed. It's a simple chord progression." She couldn't help laughing, drinking in the nearness of her sweet, strong son. Then she checked the mantel clock. "It's a quarter till six. People will start arriving any minute. Can you check the chili for me while I slice my homemade bread?"

"Sure, Mama, but it won't be as hot as your piano. You set that thing on fire!"

Jase took off for the kitchen as a knock sounded at the door. Anise turned and saw Harrison on the other side of the screen. Still in his brown pants and blue shirt from this morning, he held a big white ceramic bowl covered in plastic wrap, a tote bag, and an arrangement of creamy hydrangeas and blush-colored spray roses. His grin and twinkling summer-blue eyes made her think he'd been standing there, listening to their song, the whole time.

"Harrison, come in," she said. "Around here, if the door is open, we just call 'Anybody home?' and walk in."

"And interrupt that amazing song?" He stepped inside, and she caught a whiff of his cologne. Earthy, maybe rosemary, with a little citrus and a hint of—leather?

She moved back, giving him some room in the foyer. "It was nothing. I never had formal lessons. I just play by ear. You know, whatever I hear in my head."

He let out a low whistle of appreciation and handed her the flowers. "You might think it's nothing, but I'm impressed. My parents made me take piano lessons when I was a kid, but I made so many mistakes, you could barely recognize what I was playing."

"That's the difference between loving music and being forced to study it. My grandmother was the best piano player I ever heard, including the ones I met in Nashville when Vernon and I lived there."

His eyes widened a bit, brows raised, lips slightly parted as if he was about to speak.

But he didn't, so she turned and led the way to the kitchen. "It was just an old upright, and she'd probably had it at least fifty years, but she could make it sing."

"So she taught you to play."

"Yes, but my father was a great guitar player, and he liked for me to play when his musician friends came around to jam—when my grandmother let me. I learned a lot from him too."

Anise stopped at the butler's pantry and grabbed a vase from a cabinet there, then she swung open the kitchen door. She glanced around for Jase, but he must have stepped out to the gallery. "Mamaw Vestal instinctively understood things like the Nashville number system, but Daddy knew music theory and taught me how to make it work in a band."

He hesitated, seeming to weigh his words.

"Sounds like you have great memories, playing music at home with your family."

She chose just to smile at that and keep the reality to herself. No new acquaintance needed to hear about the amount of alcohol that had flowed during those long-ago jam sessions or how Mamaw had made Anise sleep in her room with her when the musicians stayed until the early hours of the morning. Or how Daddy's party lifestyle had driven Anise to marry way too young, mostly to escape her job in her father's bait shop/liquor store on the edge of their property. Best to leave those memories alone.

"I don't know anything about the Nashville number system, but I lived there for a year once, a long time ago." He set the bowl on the counter and the tote on the floor.

Anise dropped the arrangement into her vase and added water. "Do you sing?"

"I sang backup on the worship team at my church in San Diego, when they couldn't find anybody else. I cook better than I sing. Wait till you try my guacamole." He quickly washed his hands at the sink, dried them and pulled the plastic wrap from his bowl.

"I love guac! May I taste it? My friends' kids love it, and once they see it, it won't last five minutes."

"Sure. I hope you like it hot. I used a lot of jalapeño." He lifted a bag of chips from his tote.

Before Anise could grab a chip, Tiny Romeo let out a screech from the back gallery, where she'd set out water and food for both dogs. As his little paws scratched the door, Sugar came racing from the living room and slammed into the backs of Anise's legs as she skidded across the wood floor toward the door.

"Sugar—"

Anise lost her balance for a moment and regained it in time to stay on her feet, but the vase slipped from her hand and crashed to the floor.

For a moment, she took in the sight of glass shards and flowers, as well as the water that no doubt was seeping into the cracks of her wood floor.

"Are you okay?" Harrison took a step closer, avoiding the mess.

"I'm fine. I'll just get a broom and some rags. And another vase," she said.

"Let me sweep up the glass while you get the vase," Harrison said.

Anise pointed him toward the broom closet, then she went to the butler's pantry for another vessel. He then swept the broken glass into the dustpan while she grabbed a couple of rags from under the sink. "I hope that wasn't a special vase," he said.

"It was just a florist vase. I have only one good one, and it's in the dining room."

While he threw the glass into the waste can and washed his hands, Anise knelt and wiped up the water. Standing, with two soaked rags in her hands, she checked the time on the oven. Six o'clock. Then she caught a glimpse of the guacamole with its bright tomatoes and red onions. "Oh, no. My company will be here any minute now, and they'll empty that bowl while I'm serving supper. I won't even get a taste."

Harrison opened the chip bag. "Try it quick, before they get here."

The front door slammed hard, nearly shaking the whole house, and the sound of little feet running on the wood floor announced her friends' arrival. "Too late. Dirty hands." She held up the rags and shrugged, then hurried to the laundry room and tossed them on top of the washer.

As she headed for the kitchen sink to wash her hands, Harrison held out a giant chip loaded with guacamole. "Here you go. They'll be in here any second."

He stepped close and held it to her mouth, the blue hue of his shirt and the first rays of sunset through the big west-facing window turning his eyes an even darker shade than before.

Anise smiled at his kindness and leaned toward him—or rather, toward the guac—wary of his closeness and the scent of his cologne and the fact that no man, even her former husband, had ever fed her a bite of food. Not even at their wedding, since they'd eloped to Nashville and hadn't had a reception.

But that guac looked so perfect…

Anise bit into the chip. Closed her eyes to savor the perfect mix of smooth avocado, ripe tomatoes, onion and just the right amount of lemon juice and salt.

The kitchen door opened.

"Mama, there's a strange dog on the—"

In sync, she and Harrison swiveled their heads toward the voice.

"Mama?"

Jase. Standing in the doorway, his hand still on the knob and his eyes wide. With just one word, her son's tone had morphed from surprise to confusion to shock to—anger? Or was it disappointment?

Whichever it was, Jase wasn't happy.

Harrison backed away—far away—as she sucked in her breath, feeling like a thirteen-year-old girl who'd just been caught kissing a boy behind a tree.

Anise covered her mouth and crushed that chip between her teeth so hard, she might have broken them, then swallowed so fast it was a wonder she didn't choke.

"Uh, there's a dog...never mind." Jase turned and strode out the back door, letting Sugar out with him. Either it was Anise's imagination, or he slammed the door a little harder than usual.

Harrison moved to her side. "I'm sorry. I didn't mean to..."

"It's okay." She sighed and gazed out the kitchen window. "You just met Jase, the younger of my two sons."

She thought she saw Harrison's jaw tense a little.

"Listen, that probably looked bad. I'll go ahead home and you can call me later, once everybody's gone, and we can talk about the job."

"No, please stay. Jase has always been overprotective. It started when his father left." She smiled and touched his arm. "That's the best guac I've ever had. And Jase is a fantastic cook. You two will get along great once he understands. I'll bring him in and introduce you."

At Harrison's tentative nod, she stepped outside to the back gallery, where Jase crouched on his heels and petted the dogs.

"I'd like you to come in and meet Harrison, Jase."

Her son looked up at her, then stood, the dogs taking off across the yard. "Okay, but, Mama, you could have told me about him."

"There's nothing to tell. He just moved in

next door, and I'm considering hiring him to work with me in the mobile clinic."

Jase's eyes grew wide. "That guy's a nurse?"

"Yes, and that's all there is to it."

"I saw what was going on in there. No man feeds a woman unless—"

"Jason, listen to me." She held a firm gaze on his eyes, as she had when he was a child and had misbehaved. Then, for the first time, she realized his eyes were the exact color of Harrison's. And the same shape, with the same long, black lashes.

Not only that, but Harrison had moved from a huge city to tiny Natchez and had given up a highly specialized career to work in a job that could be boring even to a first-year nurse.

Harrison had also lived in Nashville, possibly when she and Vernon lived there, trying to make it big.

And when they'd lived there three years, her friend Starr Gray had become pregnant there by some elusive, part-time travel nurse boyfriend Anise had never met. Starr had asked Anise and Vernon to adopt their baby…

"Mama? Are you okay?"

She pushed away a few strands of hair that had fallen from her messy bun and forced her mind back to the present. "I'm fine. I understand that looked like a romantic encounter. But it wasn't. I had to wipe some water from the floor, and my hands were still dirty when we heard the kids come in. Harrison gave me a chip with guacamole because I told him I'd never get to taste it once the kids saw it."

"O-kay." He gave her that look of his, chin tucked and one eye narrowed. The look that meant he wasn't buying it.

She pushed down the hint of irritation that rose in her chest. "I have never lied to you, and I am not starting today."

He dropped his gaze. "I'm sorry. It's just that, well, it looked kind of bad."

Bad? If she'd been thirteen, maybe.

A new thought hit her: How would Jase react if she ever decided to date?

Anise dismissed the irrelevant thought. Where had it come from, anyway? "Let's go back inside. My guests are here." She hesitated, not sure she wanted her son—who was as much hers as Abe was—to meet the man who might be his father. Was he a decent man? Would he hurt Jase the way Vernon had?

She pushed aside the fears. She still didn't know he was Jase's father.

Then she remembered the words he'd written on his application.

I've learned there is something out there I want to find, and I hope to discover it in Natchez.

She felt the blood drain from her face.

"Are you okay?" Jase reached out, laid his hand on her shoulder. "You look like you're going to pass out."

No, she wasn't going to pass out. But she was pretty sure all their lives were about to change. In a way she'd never wanted.

And Harrison was here, in her home, with her entire small group present. She could hardly send him away or refuse to introduce Jase to him.

Jase had never tried to find his birth father, not wanting another disappointment after the way Vernon had treated him. So how would he react if Harrison was his father?

She drew a deep breath. Best to get it over with quickly. The lies that fear inspired were almost always worse than reality.

Inside, Harrison stood at the stove, stirring the chili in her oversized soup pot and chatting with her elder son, Abe. Looking like a young version of Vernon, Abe leaned against the counter, holding his and Rosemary's third child, three-month-old Ayla, clearly enjoying Harrison's company.

"Are you staying, Abe? Is Rosemary coming and bringing Georgia and Hollis? There's plenty of food."

"Just stopping by on the way home from

work. Rosemary and the rest of the gang are home waiting. Ayla was sleeping when she took Georgia and Hollis home, so the baby stayed in the Armstrong Kids room until I left work." Abe turned to Harrison. "My wife, Rosemary, is in charge of Armstrong Kids. It's a big room where children can play with supervision while their parents or grandparents work out."

Anise took Jase's arm, nudged him toward the stove and introduced him to Harrison, her voice a little strained, even to her ears.

Harrison set the spoon on Mamaw Vestal's "Music City" spoon holder, the souvenir Mamaw had bought on her only vacation, and extended his hand to Jase.

As Jase took it, did something change in Harrison's eyes? Or did Anise imagine it?

Chapter Two

Late that evening, with everyone else gone, Harrison sat with Anise in her living room reading nook. "I'm sorry to put a damper on your evening," he said, propping one ankle on the opposite knee.

"I'll admit it didn't go exactly as I'd expected."

He set his glass of sweet tea on the chair-side table. Next to it sat a worn leather-bound book, the author's name grasping his attention.

Elizabeth Barrett Browning.

This couldn't be a coincidence. He picked up the book and ran his finger over the engraved letters.

When he'd eavesdropped on Anise and Jase's song, he could hardly believe what he heard—his own bass voice booming at him through the screen door, only clearer, stronger. And now he was pretty sure he'd solved the mystery of

Annie's name. But seeing his own eyes glaring back at him as he met Jase, far better-looking than Harrison and twice as talented, he suspected he'd found what he'd come here for.

Lord, have I found my son?

Anise smiled. "You noticed my copy of *Sonnets from the Portuguese*. It was my grandmother's favorite, and mine too."

"The author's name intrigues me." He set the book on the table again. After the events of the evening, this would be awkward. But he had to find out if Jase was who he was looking for. "I moved here to find my son. His mother's name was Starr Gray, and the woman who adopted him was from Natchez. Her name is Annie Barrett Browning."

Her hand slid to her mouth as she dropped her gaze.

Watching the woman he believed was his son's adoptive mother, Harrison realized his weeks of making plans, renting out his house in San Diego, and getting primed to meet his last living family member hadn't begun to prepare him for this moment.

When he'd shaken Jase's hand, a strange new emotion had welled up in him, one that Trevor, his best friend, had told him about but that Harrison never dreamed he'd feel. It wasn't the protective instinct Trevor had described. But the sense of responsibility—the overwhelming desire to be there for him and help him and maybe even impart some wisdom gained from experience—was here to stay. Even if Jase would never be happy about the idea.

Then there was the other issue—Harrison had no idea how a man learned to be a father to an adult son. Even though he gave thanks to the Lord for helping him find Jase so quickly, he knew his childlessness with Lisa hadn't helped to prepare him for fatherhood.

The church bell chimed nine as he waited for Anise to confirm that she had adopted his son. Enough time passed that he started to wonder if he'd hear ten bells before she spoke.

Finally, she lifted her face and met his gaze, her eyes shimmering in the reading lamp's soft light. "I'm Annie Barrett Browning. When we lived in Nashville, Vernon somehow found us a seedy agent, and he insisted that my name wasn't a 'star' name. My grandmother used to call me Annie. Barrett is my maiden name, and I got my love of Elizabeth Barrett Browning's poetry from Mamaw. So, as unbelievable as it sounds, I'm Annie Barrett Browning."

Just as he'd thought.

He'd found his son.

Before he could express the dozens of emotions flooding him, Anise let out what sounded like a pain-filled sigh. "When I was young, I broke all three of Mamaw's rules for me, which she'd formed from her life experiences—don't mess around with alcoholic musicians, don't marry before you're eighteen and don't pretend to be someone you're not. I was definitely not Annie Barrett Browning."

Wait, what? Interesting as that was, why did Anise ramble about the past?

Then he saw it—fear hiding behind her eyes. Maybe fear of her future, now that her son had a father. Maybe fear of Jase's reaction, especially after what he'd seen in the kitchen. Or fear of the unknown, since neither Jase nor Anise knew Harrison or why he'd come to their hometown to search for him.

He had to make this easier for her if he could. "I'm sorry to spring this on you. But I'm not here to take anything from you. Or from Jase." He leaned forward in his chair, wanting nothing more at that moment than to reassure her of his intentions. "I came here to be a father to him. A real father. To help him, to love him, to be there for him. Nothing more."

"I hope so." She turned her huge brown eyes on him in a way that confirmed his responsibility to her too. He had to keep her heart safe, to make her life better instead of letting her live in fear of him and what he might do.

Maybe it was time to show her the letter.

He reached for his wallet, opened it, and pulled out the folded page. He'd read this letter so many times and had shed so many tears upon it, it was a wonder he could still read it. These words would probably remain etched in his mind until he died.

He handed it to Anise and silently recited it from memory.

It is my duty to inform you of the death of Starr Gray-Watkins, who, on her deathbed, named you as the father of the child to whom she gave birth on September 30, 1997, in Nashville, Tennessee.

Ms. Gray-Watkins confided in me that she asked Annie Barrett Browning, also of Nashville, to adopt the child. She wanted you to know the existence of your son and told me that Ms. Browning planned to take the child back to her hometown of Natchez, Mississippi, to raise.

It was Ms. Gray-Watkins's wish that you and her son know she gave him up hoping he would have a stable, happy home, which she could not provide.

Finally Anise looked up, her lashes damp. "My poor Jason. Starr could have been a good mom, if she'd given up the Nashville scene. She was so determined to become a singing sensation, nothing else mattered."

"I had no idea she was pregnant," he said, somehow needing Anise to know but wishing, for the thousandth time since he got the letter, that he'd done things differently back then. "I wouldn't have left if I'd known. I was a traveling nurse, determined to see the world, and I had an opportunity to go to Hawaii. I took it, and I never heard from Starr again."

Her eyes turned soft, a depth of emotion reflecting there. Empathy—and maybe disappointment? "Starr said you were the love of her life. But she knew you didn't feel the same."

Love of her life…

Why hadn't he considered the possibility that Starr might fall in love with him? He'd thought he made it clear to her that he lived for his career and wasn't ready for a relationship. He wanted someone to enjoy Nashville with, not to marry. But as he'd discovered with Lisa, love sometimes happens on its own schedule.

Suddenly his regret ramped up. Sure, he'd been young and fairly inexperienced at dating, but that was no excuse for thinking it was okay to have a casual relationship with a woman he'd known he'd never marry. He took a moment to thank the Lord for the long-ago Sunday morning when He revealed Harrison's embedded selfishness and began a lifelong transformation in his life and heart.

"What do we do now? A paternity test?" she asked, swiping her fingers under her eyes. "I'm not sure I'm ready to tell Jase…"

The tone of her voice suggested she wanted to add the words *until I find out more about you*.

And that was understandable. Everything in Harrison wanted to dive in and make up for lost time with his son, but that probably wasn't in anybody's best interest. "Let's get to know each other before we talk to Jase or bring up a paternity test."

"Going slow would be best for us all," Anise said, "especially since this involves more than just the three of us. Jase has a wife and daughter, and he has twins on the way. We'll know when the time is right."

A daughter… Harrison's granddaughter.

He'd realized grandchildren were a possibility. But knowing he had one made his mission that much more urgent.

"Agreed. And tomorrow's a work day for you, so I'd better head home. After I locate Tiny Romeo."

When he'd apprehended the little dog who apparently wanted a sleepover at Sugar's house, they all headed for the foyer. There Harrison stopped, turned and faced Anise. He'd have enjoyed working with this smart, intuitive woman if things hadn't become so complicated, but now, offering her a way out of their agreement seemed best.

He shifted Tiny Romeo in his arms so he could see Sugar better, and the little dog rewarded him with a couple licks on his arm. "Maybe you should get someone else to work in the mobile clinic. Like Tara said, we don't want things to be awkward."

Anise hesitated, tapping her jaw with her fingertips as if debating with herself. Or maybe praying. "On the other hand, it would give us lots of time to get to know each other," she finally said. "Besides, I need you in the clinic. If we don't start on Monday, the whole program could shut down before it starts, and Adams County's rural citizens could lose their health care."

Her dedication to the clinic—or rather, to the people the clinic could serve—shone in her eyes, making it nearly impossible for him to say no. He bit back his reservation and forced a smile that probably looked more like a grimace. "If you're good with it, so am I. I'll see you at the hospital Monday morning, then."

Having a day and time to report to work sounded good. Maybe it would at least take his mind off the fact that, at age forty-eight, Harrison had to learn to be a first-time dad to his grown son.

At Abe's invitation, Harrison pulled up to Armstrong Gym first thing on Monday to work out before his first day in the mobile clinic and to officially start his new life in his new home. Even after the events at Anise's house Thursday night, or perhaps because of them, he was ready to become a Natchezite. Permanently, if everything worked out.

Giving up the city and the only way of life he knew had been hard. But living alone in a city couldn't compare to having a son in a tiny town. Now he looked forward to becoming part of the community and building relationships.

He grabbed his gym bag from the motorcycle's top case and started inside. But before he could make it to the door, his phone rang.

Trevor. Calling to check on him, like the good friend he was. Harrison stepped away from the door and answered.

"Mitchell," Trevor said in his husky voice. "You looking for your son today?"

"I found him last night. His name is Jase Armstrong."

After a moment of what sounded like stunned silence, Trevor exploded, "Already? Dude, that's amazing. Does he look like you? What kind of man is he?"

"He's better than I could have imagined. He's a preacher, he's married and—get this—I have a granddaughter."

As Harrison filled Trevor in, his heart warmed at the fact he now had a purpose in life, other than his entire schedule revolving around work and church and hanging out with friends. For the first time in years, he had something meaningful to do with his spare time and his life. At least while Lisa was alive, he'd had someone to come home to, despite the huge strain their fertility problems had put on their marriage. Now, the only thing that made sense in his life was one day to have the kind of relationship with his son that he'd always wanted with his father.

But first Jase had to want it.

To avoid going into his embarrassing guacamole episode, he told Trevor about Anise and the mobile clinic. Trevor immediately jumped all over the fact that they were going to work together, live next door to each other and share a son. And a dog. "Anise sounds like a catch. Is she single?"

"Yeah."

"Is she cute?"

What? "I don't know. She's blond, about our age but looks younger—"

"Of course you know. Is she cute or not?"

At that moment, a red Honda scooter pulled into the parking lot. The driver got off, removed her helmet and patted her piled-up hair, looking fit in her black-and-green gym clothes.

Anise.

She caught sight of him, smiled and waved.

Oh, yeah. Anise was cute, all right. He waved back. "I guess so."

"You know, Lisa has been gone five years," Trevor said. "Why don't you ask Anise out?"

"You're not thinking straight. You know I'm nowhere close to ready for another relationship."

In fact, he wasn't even ready for a date. How could he be, when he'd made such a mess of his marriage? To this day, he couldn't figure out what he'd done that caused him always to take a back seat to the elusive, nonexistent baby that PCOS and endometriosis had robbed from Lisa. So what made him think he could ever be first in any woman's heart?

"That'll change after you've worked with Anise for a while," Trevor said as if he knew exactly how Harrison's personal life would turn out. "Speaking of work, this job will be good for you. It's about time people get to see you in action, serving and maybe even saving people right out there in the public eye instead of being the hidden helicopter hero in the background."

Naturally, his friend would try again to push Harrison into a higher-profile position, since Trevor had always thrived on the attention and the measure of local fame he'd gained through his risky rescue maneuvers.

"Nope, this is just a low-key position in a tame little country neighborhood. You know I don't like the limelight. That's why you're the fire-and-rescue guy and I'm the behind-the-scenes flight nurse. I wouldn't mind dangling at the end of a helicopter cable and saving lives like you do, but not with cameras flashing and news reporters hyping me up." He laughed. "And not wearing one of your tight T-shirts, biceps bulging."

"I wear those just for interviews. Not on the job." Trevor grinned into the phone. "If you weren't staying in Mississippi, I'd keep trying to talk you into joining my team."

"Never going to happen."

When he'd ended the call, Harrison went inside and bought a membership. With his paperwork finished and payment made, he stowed his bag in a locker and hit the cardio/weight room. Although Armstrong Gym was smaller than the one he used in San Diego, this room looked nice. The equipment was up-to-date, with treadmills, ellipticals and stationary bikes lining one long wall and weight machines along the other. He glanced around, catching sight of Anise at the leg curl machine, and started toward the weights.

Until he heard a vaguely familiar female voice calling his name.

He turned and saw Eugenia Stratton working up a sweat on the elliptical and doing a great job for a lady her age. He headed her way.

She stopped the machine and stepped off as Abe came into the weight room and spotted them.

"You were burning up that elliptical, Mrs. Stratton," Harrison said as Abe approached them, carrying an armload of folded towels.

"I've been a member of this gym since the day it opened, and I've never missed a day, except Sundays. I take the Lord's day off." She glanced toward Anise. "I'm the assistant manager at Creative Juices and Coffees next door. Why don't you and Anise stop for coffee soon? We also have some lovely blueberry kefir. And, Abe, tell your mother I've invited Harrison to our family night at Rosewood on Thursday."

Family night? "I beg your pardon, Mrs. Stratton, but you haven't invited me."

"That was your invitation." She gave him a funny, tight smile. "Be at Rosewood at six.

That's Jase's home. We eat early because of the grandchildren."

Show up at Jase's house during a family meal—without an invitation from him, or at least from Anise? He couldn't do it. Besides, by that time, she would already have put up with him for eight hours. "I'm sorry, but I don't think—"

"Nonsense. Anise will be glad you're there."

Apparently, the matter was settled, because she had decided so. She started to return to her machine, then stopped and gazed at Anise for a moment. Miss Eugenia pulled her phone from her pants pocket, worked it as if messaging someone, and headed back to the elliptical.

When she reached it, she turned around just as Anise paused from her routine and reached for her phone. She glanced at the screen, then at Miss Eugenia, and turned and met Harrison's gaze.

A little embarrassed that she'd caught him looking at her, Harrison quickly averted his eyes.

Something was up here. He could feel it. And from the forced-looking smile Anise shot his way, she knew it too.

Abe snorted out a laugh. "Miss Eugenia's got her eye on you. You'd better watch out."

"What do you mean, she's got her eye—"

"My receptionist is waving at me, probably to remind me to get to work." He slapped Harrison's back on the way out. "See you Thursday night."

Unsure how to take this new development, let alone whether or not he should attend, Harrison headed to the weights. What went on at family night, anyway? Surely, food would be involved, so he'd need to bring something to contribute. That wouldn't be hard.

The more he thought about it, the more he warmed up to the idea of getting to know Jase and the rest of the family. Besides, since neither he nor Lisa ever had relatives living close by, he'd never experienced a family night. It might be fun.

When he'd finished with the weights, his thirty-minute treadmill run and his shower, Harrison grabbed his gym bag. As he reached the door, he heard his name.

Anise.

Harrison turned and caught sight of her coming from the ladies' locker room, looking stunning in her flowing flower-print dress and mile-high wedge sandals. She wore her hair up again, a few wavy pieces framing her face.

Yeah, he sure had downplayed her looks to Trevor.

"Harrison." She smiled, the same bit of reserve in her tone that he'd heard last night, after they'd figured out Jase was his son. "Miss Eugenia texted me about her invitation to family night. I hope you'll come."

"Sure," he said, quickly making up his mind. "I appreciate it."

Clearly his son's adoptive family was close—a loving family who gathered often to eat together. But never having had such a family, would Harrison fit in? And once Jase found out about their relationship, would his son even want him there?

He could only hope so.

And for now, hope was enough.

Later that morning, Anise unlocked the RV as Harrison strode into the ER bay, wearing dark blue scrubs and a digital stethoscope and looking as if he could tackle the health problems of all of rural Adams County, Mississippi, singlehanded.

"This might be a funny question," he said, approaching the RV and invading Anise's space, "but who's going to drive this semi?"

She laughed, mentally comparing the length of the RV to an eighteen-wheeler. "I am. I took it out every day last week to get the feel of it before the clinic started."

Anise opened the RV door, then Harrison

wrestled the pull-down stairs into place and looked in. "The clinic area is separate from the cockpit?"

"There's also a door between the nurses' station and the exam room, so I can see one patient while you check in the next. Feel free to look around and make any changes you want while I do the pretravel routine."

She hopped up into the driver's seat and heard him open and close cabinet doors as she documented mileage and worked her safety protocol checklist. When she'd finished her preparations, she stepped down and walked around the vehicle and up the folding stairs.

In the freshly painted, sky-blue clinic area, Harrison had crouched down on his heels in front of the base cabinet that held emergency supplies. As Anise entered the room, he turned and faced her, looking as confident and capable as if he'd worked here for years. "Vitals cart next to the patient chair, EKG machine beside the cot, instructional materials next to the charting area—you organized everything just the way I'd do it."

He might work out fine, after all.

"Ready for takeoff?" He grinned. "Because I'm starting to get excited about your clinic."

Five minutes later, they left the city limits, Anise's stomach tightening with the excitement of the day—and maybe because working together would reveal more of Harrison's heart than she'd ever learn in a social setting. Would he be the kind of man Jase needed for a dad?

And could Anise recognize his true motives and heart? She didn't exactly have a spotless record when it came to men...

Well, to be honest, she'd had only one man in her life: Vernon. But wow, when she misjudged a man, she apparently did it epically.

"Tell me more about Jase," Harrison said, the slightest edge to his tone, as if he was half-afraid of what he might hear.

Anise couldn't help smiling as she thought of a thousand things to say about her favorite topic: her sons. "For starters, he loves Jesus with all his heart, he's the youth pastor at our church and he inherited a newborn baby two years ago when his cousin Courtney passed away unexpectedly."

Harrison's voice turned soft. "What happened to the baby's father?"

"He died before Bella was born."

"I'm sorry."

To lighten the mood, she turned the conversation back to her son. "Jase is also the Natchez Wedding Preacher, conducting destination weddings at Rosewood, a beautiful antebellum estate he manages outside of town. His family lives in the second floor of the mansion they share with his elderly boss, and he's her chef as well. He hosts youth group meetings and holiday meals too. He and Miss Fannie—his boss—invite half the town to their home on holidays. They don't want anyone to spend them alone."

"Lisa and I used to do that too, during our early years."

"Did you stop because she was sick?"

A shadow passed before his eyes, then disappeared. "After ten years of infertility, she lost the drive to reach out."

"Sometimes it's painful for an unintentionally childless woman to be around kids." She paused to breathe a quick prayer for her niece Bethany, who'd had a hysterectomy in her early twenties, due to severe endometriosis. "Did you consider adopting?"

"I suggested it, but Lisa's cousin had a bad adoption experience. The birth mother decided she wanted him back, and she got him. Lisa was always afraid that would happen to us too, so she didn't want to adopt."

"Yes, that would be hard."

"All the more reason I almost feel guilty having a child, while Lisa never did." He sat up straighter and cleared his throat. "Where are we holding our first clinic?"

The abrupt change of subject took Anise

aback for a moment, but she understood that the conversation had to be uncomfortable for him. "Today we're going to Mockingbird Creek, where I grew up," she said. "It's about a twenty-minute drive from the hospital."

"Do I sense a connection here? Does someone in Mockingbird Creek motivate you to make this clinic a success?"

"We're going there first because I wish this service had been available when my grandmother was alive." They turned onto the narrow, winding highway leading to Mockingbird Creek. "Also, since I know the people there, we'll have a good turnout. We need to make a big splash on our first day."

"I didn't expect big crowds," Harrison said as they drove through farm country. "Mobile clinics are useful in urban areas. But we haven't passed fifteen houses in the past five minutes. Will we have enough patients to make this worthwhile?"

"This is just one of the county roads our people live on. We're sparsely populated, but sixty percent of the people out here are over seventy years old." Anise made a slow, deliberate turn onto Mockingbird Creek Road. Even though she'd practiced this turn each time she took the clinic out, this sharp turn made her nervous. She hoped it didn't show. "We're holding the clinics at rural churches, and some of the members have volunteered to drive their neighbors the few miles to the clinic, whereas a trip to Natchez would take more of their time. These little towns don't have a doctor, and a lot of the elderly don't have transportation. Many of them can't drive anymore, and their families work during the day, when the offices are open. You know what happens then."

"The ER doctor becomes their family doctor."

"Right, and by the time they feel bad enough to go to the ER, their conditions are harder to treat. The other problem is insurance. You'd be surprised how many people don't have it. And if they do, they often can't afford the copay. My patients will pay five dollars per visit, and our donors make up the rest."

She glanced at him and saw that the big-city boy was getting it. "I intend to make a difference in their health and in their lives."

Harrison lifted his hand for a high five. "I think Team Anise is poised to win this clinic game."

She couldn't help grinning as she gave his palm a slap, his words inspiring more confidence in her than they should have, considering they'd just met a couple days ago. Clearly, it would be way too easy to learn to depend on Harrison, his encouragement, his authenticity—his smile…

She shut down that thought quick as a heartbeat. The last thing she needed was to develop a schoolgirl crush on her new employee. And the father of her son.

Anise flipped on the turn signal—a little too hard—and pulled into the gravel parking lot of the familiar white-frame church with its giant live oaks. A few people sat in their cars, but most of them stood under the trees or sat together on the old green-painted wooden benches. "My grandmother and I attended this little church when I was a girl. I'm thrilled to have our first clinic here."

"There must be thirty people waiting," Harrison said, leaning forward to look around.

Anise cut off the engine. "Remember that you're in the South now. Here, they'll expect you to call the older ladies 'Miss' and shake the men's hands."

An adorable confusion settled on his face. "What if the lady is married?"

She held back a laugh. "Doesn't matter. Do it like this." Anise stuck her head outside the window, waved and called out to her grandmother's former neighbor, friend and fellow church member. "Good morning, Miss Willa Mae."

The slender woman who waved back held a four-pronged cane in one hand, her familiar tight white curls grazing her shoulders as always.

While Harrison lowered the canopy and set chairs and pamphlets under it, Anise set up her tiny consultation room behind the main room where Harrison would work. When she had retrieved her otoscope, stethoscope, and blood pressure machine from a drawer and set up her laptop on the counter by the back door, she joined Harrison in the other room.

She glanced at her watch. Nine o'clock. "Ready to start?"

Harrison stood at his counter, conducting a quality control test on the glucometer. "When I'm done here, I need to document the temperature of the lab specimen refrigerator, then I can call in the first patient."

"I can get the patient," she said, heading for the door.

Miss Willa Mae Hatcher stood closest to the RV, cane in hand.

What better way to start off the new clinic than by serving her former neighbor, who was also Mamaw Vestal's close friend? "Miss Willa Mae, you're first. I'll come out and help you up the steps."

"No, I can do it." The elderly lady approached the RV, her gait fairly steady with the use of her cane, then grasped the entry's grab bar and started up the two steps.

But before Anise knew what was happening,

Miss Willa Mae toppled forward on the stairs as if she'd lost her balance, catching herself with one hand.

The back door opened and slammed shut, and within moments, Harrison was outside and taking charge.

"Miss Willa Mae, I'm Harrison Mitchell, the nurse," he said in a soothing voice. "Are you hurt?"

"I think I'm okay."

Harrison had pulled on a pair of blue latex gloves, probably as he ran around the RV. From the side, he swiveled Miss Willa Mae's body a little and then faced her, slid his arms under hers and lifted her to a standing position on the ground. "Do you feel well enough to go in and have your appointment?"

She nodded, and that's when Anise noticed blood dripping from a laceration on the back of her hand.

She tugged on a pair of gloves and cleaned the blood from the older lady's hand, then helped her inside.

Moments later, Harrison came in the back door and met the women at the nurses' station.

"I got blood all over your shirt when you lifted me," Miss Willa Mae said, pointing.

"No problem. I have on another shirt underneath." As Anise settled Miss Willa Mae in the patient chair, Harrison looked down at the red spots, then he peeled off his gloves, pulled a red biohazard bag from under the sink, and threw them in. Then he washed his hands and carried the bag to the consultation room.

Within moments, he was back, wearing a blue T-shirt with his scrub pants. He cleaned the laceration and applied a bandage.

"I'm here about my blood pressure," Miss Willa Mae said, pulling a home blood pressure cuff from her oversized orange purse. "It gives me a different number each time I take it. The doctor said I have to take it every day because I had a stroke last year. It affected my left leg."

"Show me how you do it," he said.

Within five minutes, Harrison had Miss Willa Mae using the machine correctly.

"You're the best doctor in Natchez!" she said.

"Thank you, but I'm a nurse. Anise is the nurse practitioner, and she works like a doctor."

The elderly lady's laughter rang through the RV. "I went to her college graduation—from nursing school. Not medical school. She's not a doctor. She's a nurse."

Anise smiled. "You're right, Miss Willa Mae. I'm a nurse."

After her appointment, Harrison helped the elderly lady up and to the door. She tried to take the first step, but every time she lifted her foot, she froze.

"I'm scared of these narrow metal steps. Going down is worse than coming up."

"Put your arms around my neck," Harrison said, taking her left hand and settling the weaker arm on his shoulder. "I'm going to carry you down those stairs, okay?"

Miss Willa Mae nodded.

"I'll go down first and help if you need it," Anise said as she hurried down the steps to the churchyard.

Harrison slid one arm under Miss Willa Mae's knees, lifted her and started for the door.

On the way down the steps, giggling and squealing like a teenager, she patted his cheek. "Did y'all see that?" she called to her friends under the trees and the RV's canopy. "Handsomest doctor in Mississippi just swept me off my feet!"

Harrison's laugh rang through the churchyard, his smile big and natural-looking.

Yes, handsome was definitely one way to describe Anise's new nurse. And she couldn't pretend she hadn't noticed the way his shirt strained under his muscular shoulders as he carried Miss Willa Mae down the steps as easily as if she were one of Anise's grandchildren. But more than that, he exuded such a caring attitude that she couldn't help wondering if he might learn to love Jase like a father someday. And be a grandfather to Jase's daughter, Bella, and the babies on the way.

Anise would definitely keep her eye on him.

On his behavior, that is. Not on his beautiful eyes and strong shoulders.

Six hours later, the parking lot was empty.

"I checked in forty-four patients," Harrison said, rolling up the canopy. "Got two EKGs, drew twelve tubes of blood, extracted a tick from a scalp, and flushed wax out of an ear."

"We finished a little earlier than I anticipated. What would you think of adding one more patient—a house call?" she asked before they drove off.

He paused. "That would be different."

"It's a bedridden thirteen-year-old boy named Colton Powell. A couple of months ago, he had a four-wheeler accident that left him with spinal fracture–induced paralysis, and his mama can't get him to town to see a doctor. They have a home health nurse, but I'd still like to check in and see how they're both doing, since they're members of our church."

Harrison's eyes turned steely for a moment, his jaw tightening.

What had caused that? She waited a moment

for him to speak, but he seemed to have retreated into a memory. "If you'd rather not—"

"No." Most of the tension left his face as he met her gaze across the cockpit. "Let's go."

"Only if you're sure. They live about five miles from here, toward town. It shouldn't take long."

"I'm sure," he said, conviction in his deep voice. "Maybe we can help."

Minutes later, she and Harrison drove up the quarter-mile-long driveway to the house. Inside, they assessed Colton as he lay in the living room recliner, his mama, Krystal, by his side.

"You've got some yellow gunk around your trach, Colton." Harrison turned to Krystal. "Even though the button is on now, and he's breathing naturally, he needs good trach care three times a day to prevent infection."

They watched her cleanse the area with saline and sterile cotton swabs, and Harrison gave her a few tips for keeping it clean. Then he and Anise turned Colton over and checked his skin for pressure sores, and found none.

"I might walk down to the mailbox while you're here to sit with Colton," Krystal said. "I don't like to leave him alone."

When she'd left, Harrison pulled a kitchen chair next to the recliner and sat with Colton, chatting about their common interests of football and weightlifting.

"What do you want most right now, buddy?" Harrison asked. "Other than walking."

Colton's green eyes clouded. "I want my mama to not have to work so hard. If I hadn't raced into the creek and turned over the four-wheeler..." He averted his face.

Oh, Jesus, help Colton... Anise stepped into the kitchen, still able to see and hear them but out of Colton's line of vision.

Harrison let out a big breath. "You didn't mean to do this. And your mom wants to work hard and give you the care you need. Don't let yourself feel guilty."

"How am I supposed to not feel guilty? My dad left after the accident, and Mama quit her job so she can stay with me. She hasn't left since I came home from the hospital."

Harrison looked around the room. "Do you have a Bible?"

"It's on the coffee table. Mama reads it to me every night."

Harrison grabbed it, opened it to the page he wanted and held it so Colton could see. Then he pointed to a line. "Here's a verse that helped me once when I felt guilty. At least, it's part of a verse. 'Bringing into captivity every thought.' That means we don't have to let our minds wander anywhere they want. When you start to feel guilty, capture that thought and get rid of it."

Colton's eyes grew misty, and he blinked fast. "I will."

When a few tears ran down Colton's face, Harrison reached for a tissue from the table next to the bed and wiped the boy's cheeks. Then he cupped Colton's chin. "You can do it. I'll stop in and see you again, buddy."

When they returned to the RV, dusk had begun to fall, giving the evening a lonely undertone. After several minutes, Harrison shifted in his seat, half facing Anise.

"I think more could be done for Colton. How often are you scheduled to come to Mockingbird Creek?"

"Twice a week," she said, sensing a change in him. She didn't know what, but something about Colton had affected him—a lot.

He hesitated. "I used to be the most impulsive guy you've ever met. In time, I learned self-control. But I also learned when I needed to take quick action."

"What action?"

Harrison's jaw tightened. "Colton reminds me of someone. So does his mom."

"What do you want to do?"

"I want to work in this shabby gas hog of a clinic with you instead of the ER."

She caught her breath. "Permanently?"

He nodded. "If you'll have me."

"Are you sure? This isn't nearly challenging enough for you. And you could make better money in the ER."

"I'm not worried about the money. My late wife and I both worked hard and saved all these years, and we never had children to spend our money on, so I have enough. I believe in what you're doing, and I want to be a part of it."

"And that way you can see Colton?"

"Maybe we can help him have a better quality of life if we discover what other mobile clinics are doing for kids like him." He fixed his deep blue gaze on her. "Besides, this whole area is ours to care for, right?"

Anise held out her hand. "Deal."

Maybe she wasn't the best judge of character when it came to the men in her life. But it sure seemed as if they couldn't have found a better mobile clinic nurse than Harrison Mitchell.

Chapter Three

Anise could sit here for the rest of the day and relish the emails, social media hits and newspaper stories congratulating her on the clinic's impact.

Back in the office, she had collapsed into her chair and now spun to face Harrison, sitting at his desk. With their daily reports done, she grabbed her tablet and pulled up the clinic's social media.

"Check this out," she said, rolling her chair over to his. "I never dreamed we'd get this kind of exposure and support."

He took it and scrolled through clinic pictures she'd posted over lunch, along with tagged photographs from patients. "Me either. These comments are amazing. You've gained an impressive following and a lot more support."

"Look at this." She leaned over and swiped

the screen, revealing a newspaper article and picture of Harrison carrying Miss Willa Mae down the RV's stairs. The caption read *New Rural Mobile Clinic Nurse Sweeps Patients Off Their Feet.*

"What? Who wrote that? Who took that picture? I look like a gorilla."

Anise laughed at the embarrassment in his voice and the flush in his face. "Cassius Cole from the *Natchez Courier* took it. It's nothing to be ashamed of. In fact, your smile is infectious. Cassius must have snapped it when you were laughing at Miss Willa Mae's joke about you sweeping her off her feet. It's a good picture."

"If we were running a zoo, then yes."

"You look buff, that's all." She couldn't resist telling him the fun part. "Check the comments. You have about fifteen date offers and at least one marriage proposal."

He rolled his eyes. "Great. Now we've gone from a clinic to a zoo to an online dating service."

His mock scowl made her laugh again. In fact, Harrison had made her laugh a lot today, which felt good after so many years with no one to joke with.

Her text message notification sounded from within her purse, so she pulled out her phone and saw Miss Eugenia's profile picture of herself with Georgia, Hollis and Ayla—three of Anise's grandchildren and all of Miss Eugenia's great-grandchildren. Anise scanned the message.

I've seen your clinic all over social media. The whole family is going to Vestal's Flower Farm tonight at five for a celebration. Make sure Harrison comes. Eugenia Price Mabel Stratton.

She let out a deep sigh. *Miss Eugenia...*

"What's wrong?" Harrison asked, his concern thick in his voice.

"Nothing. It's just—" She handed him the phone. If he knew that Anise suspected Miss Eugenia of being the famed, mysterious Natchez matchmaker who'd never failed to make a match, and that it looked as if she had her eye on Anise and Harrison, he'd head back to San Diego before they had a chance to tell Jase about him.

Which might not be so bad...

"She signs her full name to her text messages?"

"Miss Eugenia has a lot of quirks," Anise said. "But we can't celebrate on our first day."

"I disagree with the faulty logic. Why wait?"

"If we celebrate today, what will we do if everything falls apart tomorrow?"

"We'll be glad we had a good time and served

a lot of people. What's the worst thing that could happen at the celebration?"

Jase realizing how much he looks like you and guessing the truth before I'm ready. "I guess...my hopes being dashed later."

"Not going to happen. What's the best thing?"

"I'll get to spend time with my sons and grandchildren."

"See? You'll have a great evening. Where is the flower farm, and why did she choose it for the celebration?"

"It's my favorite place in the world. It was my grandmother's business and home. Since my siblings all live up north and never wanted the farm, it's mine now. The business shut down after she died, but the family goes there for picnics." For a moment, she let her mind drift back to Mamaw Vestal and her love of flowers. "We were close to it today. It's near Mockingbird Creek Church."

The look in Harrison's eyes told her how much he wanted to go.

Despite her fears, she didn't want to defy Miss Eugenia.

"We'll barely have time to make it by five," she said, glancing at her watch.

"Then it's a good thing I have the prep work done for another batch of guacamole. It won't take five minutes to peel and mash the avocadoes, drain the tomatoes and put everything together."

Well, that certainly sweetened the deal. Or would have, if it wasn't for their earlier guac fiasco... "Ride with me, and let's take the dogs. Abe installed an invisible fence when I got Sugar, and it came with two collars, so Tiny Romeo can wear one."

"Now that I'm a dog owner, I guess I'll have to get a car," he said. "Can't put Tiny Romeo on my Harley."

An hour later, they piled Sugar, Tiny Romeo, and a big bowl of guac and chips into Anise's Jeep and headed back out of town. Soon they pulled into Mamaw's weedy driveway, behind Jase's vintage Mustang, the SUV Abe and Rosemary had just bought for their growing family, and Rosemary's parents' little hybrid car. As Anise caught sight of the home she'd grown up in, the old nostalgia hit her again. But the problem with nostalgia was the way it often used good memories to mask the bad.

Harrison grabbed Tiny Romeo and the guac while Anise managed Sugar and the tote full of chips.

"I wish I could maintain the whole yard and all the flower gardens the way my grandmother did. Other than the yard and house—and the spot where Daddy's trailer used to be—the entire five acres of cleared ground used to be the flower farm." She cast a glance at the decrepit building on the corner. "Besides the bait store, of course."

Seeing it again stirred up the old memories— bad memories—she tried hard to forget.

"Have you considered fixing it up and re-opening it?" he asked.

"I'd rather tear it down. We called it the bait store, but it was also a liquor store and the place where local musicians gathered to jam. And drink."

"Nannie!" Six-year-old Georgia, Anise's oldest grandchild, bounded up to her, breaking the hold of the past. The little girl stopped when she saw Harrison.

"Who's that?" she asked, pointing.

"Remember, we don't point, and we politely ask people their names." Anise picked up her granddaughter and settled her on her hip. "You can call him Mr. Harrison."

"That's a funny name for a dog," Georgia said, twisting one of her long, dark curls around the crayon in her hand.

"I'm Harrison," he said, a twinkle in his eye, "and this is Tiny Romeo."

Georgia's one-year-old brother, Hollis, toddled up and raised his hands to Anise. She bent over and managed to pick him up too. Never happier than when her arms were full of her grandchildren, she kissed Hollis on his cheek, still a bit sticky as if he'd been eating his favorite food: jelly bread. "This is Hollis, my third grandchild."

Harrison high-fived the toddler. "How many more do you have?"

"Just these two, their baby sister, Ayla, whom you saw at my house, and Jase's two-year-old, Bella. And, of course, his twins are due in a month. So four here, two soon to come. My heart is full, and my arms often are too." She paused and looked at Georgia, who baby-talked to Tiny Romeo, reaching out her arms to him.

Anise set Georgia down and Harrison handed Tiny Romeo to her. But the little dog immediately wriggled, wanting down.

Probably because his lady dog, Sugar, was nearby.

Hollis wanted to join his sister and the dogs, so she set him down too.

"Bella, wait."

Harrison turned toward Jase, who chased after Bella. Seeing the longing and anticipation in Harrison's eyes, Anise had to turn away for a moment.

Unbidden, a memory flashed into her mind: the day Abe and Rosemary brought then three-year-old Georgia to see Anise for the first time. She'd been in her reading nook, the very spot where she'd sat with Harrison, talking about Jase. Abe had handed the little girl to her, changing her life, her world—her heart—forever.

Georgia had called her Miss Anise.

And it had pierced her heart. Because all Anise had wanted at that moment was to hear the sweet little girl call her Nannie or Grandma or even Grandmother. Not Miss Anise.

But Harrison? Would he want Bella to call him Grandpa?

No, he didn't seem like a Grandpa. He'd probably choose Papaw, Papa or even Pappy.

Whatever name the little girl called him, he had as much right to a relationship with Bella as Anise did.

Lord, give me a right heart about this...

Jase scooped up Bella and headed toward them, prompting a few tears from the little girl. Behind him, Miss Eugenia spread vintage flowered tablecloths on the picnic tables Abe had set under the biggest Southern live oak last year. Rosemary's mother, Cozette, handed out water and soft drinks while her husband, Judge Wilson, visited with Miss Fannie Swan, a close family friend and Jase's employer.

From the tree branches, swaying in the gentle evening breeze, hung a white banner that looked like an old sheet painted with a colorful misspelled greeting—Congatuatons. No doubt

Georgia's work. Someone, probably Miss Eugenia, had decorated the area with pumpkins, hay bales, flint corn, and red and yellow mums. With both dogs and the children running free, Mamaw Vestal's Flower Farm seemed like the happiest place in Adams County.

But even happy places sometimes had dark pasts.

"Erin and Miss Fannie think Bella's second molars are coming in," Jase said as he handed the dark-haired girl to her. "She's been fussy since yesterday."

Wait, did Jase just ignore Harrison?

She gave her son what the boys used to call "the look."

"You remember Harrison, Jase?"

"Uh, yeah. Sorry. Hi, Harrison." He hesitated then wiped his hand on his pant leg and held it out. "Hope you don't mind a little baby spittle."

"Not in the least." Harrison's smile looked so sincere, so hopeful, as he clasped his son's hand, it brought a tear to Anise's eye.

Why did everything have to be so complicated?

Harrison knew without a doubt that he'd never forget this moment as long as he lived.

Never mind that Jase had snubbed him. He'd mull that over later. Because now he was catching his first glimpse of his granddaughter.

His granddaughter.

And what a beauty. Dark hair, delicate features, big blue eyes that shone in the brilliance of the last bright rays of late-afternoon sun.

And that feeling of protectiveness he'd missed when he first met Jase? The one Trevor said could stop a man's heart, make him a hero willing to lay down his life?

Oh, yeah. That feeling hit him now like a punch to the gut.

He'd never felt anything so surreal. So powerful.

Harrison swallowed back the lump in his throat, that intangible, indescribable force that demanded he be here for this kid, in every sense of the word, as long as he lived.

Wow, he hadn't expected this.

Then he realized he had no idea how long he'd stood there, silent, lost in the wonder and fear of it all while Anise and Jase probably wondered what was wrong with him.

Harrison swallowed again, not knowing another way to gain control, and resisted the urge to touch the little hand that reached out to him, not sure that Jase would want him to.

"This is Bella. Jase and Erin's daughter," Anise said, and he realized the hour that had just passed had really been only a few seconds. "You can take her hand if you want to."

"I… I don't have much experience with babies." He took the tiny hand anyway, holding it gently in his fingertips.

And Bella smiled at him.

His sudden love for this baby surged through his heart. If he'd thought he'd been overemotional before…

"Don't worry," Jase said, his tone suddenly tender. "When Bella came into my life, I knew less than nothing about being a father. I got custody of her when she was three days old, and I had never held a baby before. If I hadn't had Mama, Erin and Miss Fannie, I wouldn't have made it past the first hour."

"Jase, you wouldn't have made it past the first minute." Anise's warm, smiling eyes flitted from Jase's face to Harrison's, giving him a little much-needed grounding.

Miss Eugenia, who pulled off a youthful vibe in her straight light-blue jeans, a Way Maker long-sleeved T-shirt and tan suede sneakers, waved them to the tables. But those tables were piled with so much food, Harrison wasn't sure the guests would have room for their plates.

"Congratulations on your first day, Harrison and Anise," Miss Eugenia said after her family quieted down and she had introduced Harrison. "Since even Jase couldn't put together a meal for this crowd on such short notice, we brought red beans and rice with andouille from Farrah's, caprese salad and Cajun shrimp from Pearl Street Pasta, and hummingbird cake, banana caramel pie and coconut cream pie from the Cupboard. And Harrison brought his famous guacamole. Y'all bow your heads. Harrison, give thanks to the Lord."

Whoa, he hadn't expected that. Especially so abruptly. And what did she mean by "famous guacamole"?

However, he knew she was honoring him by asking him to pray, especially with a minister at the table. So, recovering in a flash, he changed his focus and invited the Lord's presence at the meal, thanked Him for the food and the invitation and, as a last thought, for the blessing of family and friends.

He wanted to say more, to express his gratitude for the son and granddaughter God had allowed Harrison to discover so quickly. But he gave silent thanks for those matters instead and said his amen.

As bowls passed from hand to hand, Abe piped up from across the table. "It was nice to hear somebody else pray besides Jase all the time," he said, grinning at his brother. "Mama always chooses him to pray. But non-preachers know how to pray too."

"Maybe she chooses me because *some* people don't know when the prayer should end because the food is getting cold," Jase said in a mock grumble from the other side of the table, his eyes twinkling. "When *some* people pray, we cover everything from orphanages to the economy to finding cures for deadly diseases. Then we put our plates in the microwave."

"Changing the subject..." Miss Eugenia said. "That was quite the picture of you on social media today, Harrison. I never saw Willa Mae smile so big, and I've known her my whole life."

Miss Eugenia had seen that picture?

He groaned inwardly. The last thing he wanted was for that terrible picture to circulate. He'd hoped—even prayed—that no one in Jase's family had seen it, other than Anise.

He had to make sure Trevor never saw this picture, since he wanted Harrison to have a high-profile position. And while he didn't have that, he sure had the flashing camera and hyped-up headline.

The moment he saw that picture, he knew he looked a little like Trevor, in a heroic pose, panning for the camera. But what worked for Trevor didn't work for Harrison. Trevor's pictures of his rescues endeared him to people, encouraged them to support the fire-rescue team. Harrison's picture, on the other hand, looked like he was drawing attention to himself, putting on a show. Showing off.

He blew out a breath. If only he hadn't worn that too-tight T-shirt...

He glanced at Anise, who sat on his other side, and shrugged. "I guess even a bad picture can be good publicity."

"Are you kidding?" Abe said, his eyes wide. "I'm going to buy a copy of that picture from the newspaper. Then I'm going to frame it and hang it in my gym. You're famous in Natchez now, and since you work out at my place—"

This couldn't be happening...

"Wait a minute," Jase interrupted his brother, puzzlement in his eyes. "What picture?"

"It's nothing. Just a candid shot of me helping a patient."

This could get ugly—Harrison could feel it. The picture itself was bad enough, with his biceps bulging and his shirt stretched tight across his shoulders and him holding Miss Willa Mae as if she were Fay Wray. Sort of. But Anise had said the comments included date offers and—

And at least one marriage proposal...

He groaned, remembering Anise's words. How many proposals? And why had those women done such a nonsensical thing, just when he was trying to make a good impression on Jase?

"I want to see that picture," Jase said, sounding like the suspicious father of a rebellious teenage girl.

"Jase, it's nothing…"

Abe pulled out his phone. "Here ya go. I set it as the gym's profile picture on social media."

No…

Everything inside Harrison wanted to jump up and grab that phone as Abe passed it to Jase. But the phone made its way down the table, with Abe's dark-haired wife, Rosemary, swiping the screen to see the picture first. Her eyes went wide, and she stared at Harrison for a moment and then passed the renegade phone to Erin, Jase's blond wife. Erin merely covered her grin with her hand and gave the phone to Jase.

Harrison couldn't watch. He fumbled around with his fork, then gave up spearing anything on his plate and grabbed a tortilla chip instead, loaded it with as much guacamole as he could fit on it and lifted it to his mouth.

"That's…quite a show, Harrison."

At Jase's words, Harrison looked up and made eye contact with his son just as he bit into that giant guacamole chip.

Could this "celebration" possibly get any worse?

Chapter Four

Dusk fell on the bayou, bringing a chilly September breeze from the creek, as the little party prepared to disperse. Before long, on this rock road with no houses within a mile of the flower farm, bright stars would begin to shine.

Anise shivered a little, and not because of the wind. In town, twilight didn't bother her. But out in the deeper darkness of the bayou, dusk still gave her a sense of unease.

Growing up here, she'd thought the twilight foreboding, especially when Daddy's friends started to stir and make their way to the rickety old store, where their music mellowed with each drink. Of course, Anise heard it only through the open window of her grandmother's bedroom, since Mamaw always shooed her inside as soon as the first shades of dusk fell.

But those days were long gone.

Apparently, Anise was the only leery one here tonight. Harrison hadn't looked the slightest bit overwhelmed during supper, though his emotions had to have run high as he spent time with what was essentially his new family. Even if he and Anise were the only ones who knew it.

And he'd certainly handled Jase's mild rudeness with grace.

Now he played some kind of running game with Georgia near the flower field, touching the top of her head and then dropping and rolling on the damp grass as the little girl shrieked with laughter.

The man was a natural with kids.

And seemed not to know it.

Anise caught herself smiling at their antics until she saw Jase's slight frown as he watched them. Sure as the sunset, he was still sizing Harrison up. As she watched, that frown embedded itself deeper into Jase's forehead and between his eyes.

She ambled toward him and took sleeping Bella from him to give his arms a rest. The two-year-old roused only enough to bury her sweet face in Anise's neck. "Got time to talk?"

"Sure. Erin will want to go soon, though." He glanced at his wife, displaying the charming expectant-father demeanor Anise had watched develop in him the past few months.

As Georgia barreled toward them, they stepped back, mindful of the little girl's propensity to run headlong first and look around later. Anise laid her free hand on Jase's shoulder. "You seem a little tense tonight."

His breath came out in a puff as he shifted his rather stony focus to Harrison. "Yeah, I guess I am."

As much as she dreaded it, she needed to ask. "Want to tell me why?"

He seemed to rip his gaze from Harrison and then fixed it on Anise instead, the uncharacteristic hardness melting. "I'm not used to seeing you with a man. If he was from around here, someone we know and trust, that would be one thing. But we know nothing about this guy, except that he can carry heavy objects. And that a lot of women on social media would like to go out with him. And marry him."

Anise chose not to comment on the fact that Miss Willa Mae was not an object. And he was right—three more women had crafted social media "proposals" after the first one. "I doubt they were serious. Besides, that wasn't Harrison's fault. Miss Willa Mae couldn't walk down the RV stairs, and he helped her. It was sweet."

"Mama, this is the first time in my life I've heard you call a man sweet."

"Yes, but—"

"It's none of my business who you—date." Jase said the word *date* in the same tone he might use if he were speaking of a dirty diaper left in the trash can too long. "But I'm not used to this. It was just the three of us for so long, this is hard to wrap my mind around."

His deep blue eyes held a trace of cynicism and a depth of pain she hadn't seen in them for years.

She hesitated, the night birds singing the first lines of their mournful songs.

Time to come in the house, Annie. Night birds are callin'.

Mamaw Vestal's evening admonition rolled through Anise's memory, igniting once again that long-ago sunset melancholy, the decades-old fear of what might happen after dark.

She scanned the area—the yard, the road, the now-blackening woods—her senses alert to the nameless danger Mamaw had always protected her from as if it were her calling.

Anise shivered.

Maybe it had been.

Jase's gentle touch on her arm helped shake off the unreasonable fear and dispel her dark recollections. They were safe. Unsavory characters didn't gather here after dusk as they once had.

And no one called her Annie anymore.

"Mama, are you okay?" her son said. "Ever since that guy showed up, you've been acting kinda funny."

Well, she wasn't the only one.

"I'm fine. But there's something you're not telling me—some reason you don't like Harrison."

Jase lifted his hand from her arm. "You're right. I don't like him."

"Why not?"

He looked at Harrison again, his face pinched into an unnatural scowl. "He's a city slicker, and he's after my mama."

City slicker? Who said that anymore? Had they just time-warped back to 1930?

But, glancing at Harrison, she had to admit his dark-wash jeans, heather-colored cashmere sweater, upscale white tennis shoes and vintage, high-end wristwatch—at a picnic—didn't exactly shout small town.

"Okay, I'll admit he dresses differently than most Natchez men." She glanced at Jase's faded jeans and blue River Church sweatshirt. But the part about Harrison being after Anise…

"How long have you known him, anyway? Did you meet before he came here?" He hesitated. "Maybe online?"

She tensed, partly because it was both ridiculous and a little annoying for her son to interrogate her about a man. Also because she'd never considered meeting a man online. "I met him this past Thursday, the same day you did. I don't know what I'll have to do to convince you that we're just friends. Just coworkers, really."

He laid his hand on her shoulder, the way he used to do when he was a boy and occasionally caught her weeping over Vernon's betrayal. "I might feel better about this if you'd simply admit you're interested in each other instead of pretending you're not."

Anise stifled the sigh that wanted to escape her lips. Nothing she could say would convince Jase that she had zero romantic interest in Harrison, and that Harrison had even less interest in her. And as long as Jase thought otherwise, he wouldn't give Harrison half a chance.

Erin came over then, a sweet maternal waddle in her gait, probably to relieve Anise of the weight of the toddler she held.

Sure enough, when Erin reached her, she held out her arms. "I'll take a turn with her."

"She won't tire you too much?" Anise glanced at Erin's so-very-pregnant abdomen. She'd never make it another month.

"Let me carry her, Erin," Jase said, reaching for the little girl.

Anise kissed her granddaughter's soft cheek and received a slobbery one in return, then

Jase's little family headed for their car. As they drove away, one thing was sure—Jase was nowhere near ready to learn that Harrison was his birth father.

Light footsteps approached behind her, and she turned to see Miss Eugenia, holding two bundles of red, yellow and purple flint corn, held together with a piece of jute. "Fannie and I plan to take these and the smaller mums to Joseph Duncan tomorrow. We thought he needed some autumn cheer, but the straw bales and the big mums should go to the church. You and Harrison can pick them up tomorrow after work, right? You'll have plenty of room in that RV."

A twinge of apprehension brought in Anise's focus. What had happened to cause their lifelong friend to need cheering? "Is Joseph all right?"

"He fell and sprained his ankle this afternoon."

And, of course, Miss Eugenia had found out about it. "How did it happen?"

"He somehow twisted his foot while he was planting ornamental cabbage and purple chard in Frieda's fall flower garden." She closed her eyes and tipped her head for a moment as she and her older lady friends often did when speaking of the deceased. "He's getting too old for that. I'm going to find someone to do his gardening for him. Although he needs a wife. Frieda's been gone since the summer you were born."

Anise returned the gesture as was expected but ignored the wife comment. "Can I do anything to help?"

"Just take those mums and bales to the church before choir practice tomorrow. I need them to decorate the foyer the next day. I have Joseph under control."

Yes, Anise could imagine she did. "I'm not sure we can close the clinic, pick up the straw bales and mums, and get back to town by then. Besides, I park in the ER bay and wouldn't want to explain to the staff why I'm late getting the RV back. Or tell the housekeeping staff why they have to clean straw out of it."

Miss Eugenia smiled and nodded as she strode toward Judge Wilson's car, where the judge and Cozette waited in the front seat. "Then park the RV and borrow Abe's truck."

"But I don't drive a stick shift." She quickstepped to catch up. "And Abe can't take me because he'll still be at work. He can't take them now either, because all these bales and mums won't fit in his SUV with Erin and all three children in it."

"Then borrow his truck and have Harrison drive it. After you deliver the decorations, you can both stay for choir practice. Harrison has a wonderful voice."

What? "When did you hear Harrison sing?"

"He sat behind me in church yesterday. He can read music too."

"He couldn't have been at church. I would have seen him."

"You didn't see him because he and Pastor David were talking in the office before the service. And when he came into the sanctuary, you were working in the nursery," Miss Eugenia said as if she'd been keeping a log of Harrison's comings and goings. "You didn't see him leave because you had to change Bella's diaper just as the service ended. Georgia told me about the diaper blowout."

Apparently, even six-year-olds were now part of Miss Eugenia's spy network. "But how do you know Harrison can read music?"

"Easy. You know how 'Leaning on the Everlasting Arms' has that strange bass harmony line in our hymnal? The one the choir has to practice over and over because all the men are used to singing it the regular way?" Miss Eugenia waited for Anise's nod. "Harrison sang it right the first time through, which means he can not only read music, but he can sight read too. He'll make a great addition to the choir."

Honestly, did anything in Natchez ever escape

Miss Eugenia's eye—and ear? And was no un-
attached person between the ages of eighteen
and eighty safe from her meddling?

While she appreciated the older lady's concern for Harrison and her desire to help him fit
into Natchez, Anise had no intention of letting
Miss Eugenia play the matchmaker for her. Not
with Harrison, and not with any other man. Her
main concern in life right now was the tension
between Jase and Harrison.

But as Judge Wilson, Miss Cozette and Miss
Eugenia pulled out of the driveway, Anise realized the older woman didn't care when those
fall decorations got to church. Her only motivation had been to throw Anise and Harrison
together—again. Just as this "celebration" was
merely a matchmaking ploy.

The irony hit her—Miss Eugenia wanted
them together as much as Jase wanted them
apart.

And exactly how did you fight a force as
strong as Eugenia Price Mabel Stratton?

She caught Harrison's gaze just as Georgia
bounded away to answer her mother's call. He
jogged across the yard toward Anise in time to
get a goodbye hug from Georgia and a handshake from Abe before his family piled into the
van and left for home.

"It's funny that Abe and I hit it off the moment we met, but Jase…" A twinge of longing colored Harrison's voice. But when he looked at her, his gaze bore into her eyes as if he could see into her heart, into her growing exasperation with Jase and her fear of his reaction when he learned the truth. "What's wrong? Did something just happen with Jase?"

Anise massaged the pounding that started between her eyebrows. Nothing within her wanted to hurt Harrison, but he needed to know how Jase felt.

Although he certainly did not need to know how Miss Eugenia felt.

"Things aren't going too well with Jase," she said.

"Something's wrong between you two? Because I never wanted—"

"No." She rubbed her aching forehead. "Yes. We're okay. It's just—I can't convince Jase that you and I aren't dating. He thinks we're secretly having a relationship, and he's upset that I didn't tell him. And to be honest, I'm hurt that he doesn't trust me."

Harrison's eyes turned humble, almost contrite. "His protective nature is making a mountain out of it and keeping him from giving me a chance. I don't know how he'll react when he finds out the truth."

Neither did Anise.

At that moment, all she wanted was to grab her son and shield him from the hurt and harm that might come to him if Harrison didn't turn out to be the man she hoped—prayed—he was.

Jase—the sweet little boy who'd wept for days when his father left them without a word, without a hint he was leaving, without a good-bye or a handshake or a hug.

The brave older boy who'd insisted last year's school clothes were good enough and that, instead of buying new jeans for him, she put her few dollars toward the debt his father had left behind.

The devoted teenager who'd waited up for her to get home from the Natchez Nursing Center every night, curled up on the old tattered couch they'd dragged home from the side of the road after the good furniture Vernon bought on credit had been repossessed.

The young man who'd made her prouder than she thought she could ever be when he adopted his cousin's orphaned newborn.

Jesus, he's been through so much, and one father has already betrayed him. If Harrison would hurt him the same way...

She stopped the thought cold. If his humble, seemingly heartfelt mealtime prayer was any indication, Harrison was a man who loved Jesus. And although Anise had known him only a short time, she hadn't detected pride, arrogance or selfishness. All she'd seen him do since he came into their lives was give of himself.

Still, as Jase had pointed out, none of them knew much about Harrison. For all they knew, he could still turn out to be as untrustworthy and as unfaithful as Vernon.

She thought back to the days after Vernon left, when, in despair, she'd given her life to Jesus and He gave her an intuitiveness she hadn't had before. Pastor David said it was discernment. Whatever they called it, she'd begun to sense, among other things, wrong motives or poor character in some of the men who came her way. That sense had never failed her.

But now, as she looked into Harrison's clear blue eyes, she wasn't sure what she saw. Was she ignoring potential red flags because she wanted him to be the father Jase needed—the grandfather Bella and the new babies needed? Or was she raising her own flags because of her family's history of pain and betrayal?

"I don't know how long to wait before we tell him who I am." Harrison set his gaze on the now-orange sky as if looking there for answers, as Anise was. "If we wait too long, he could be angry that we kept the news from him."

"But if we tell him now, he might cut you out altogether."

"There's only one solution, Anise." He pulled his attention from the sunset. "We have to get the viewpoint of the Lord on this. The timing must be right, and so does my behavior. Every time I turn around, I inadvertently do something that looks bad to him. That needs to stop."

And just like that, Harrison grasped her hand and started a prayer with an intensity that nearly took her breath away. Never in her life had she heard anyone pray for her family as Harrison did at this moment.

Anise agreed with him in prayer, adding her own silent petitions to his, but fear soon hit her again.

Lord, I need to know what kind of man Harrison is. Will he be a good father to Jase—the kind of man he and his children need?

The only answer she sensed in her heart was the scripture *All things work together for good to them that love God, to them who are the called according to His purpose.*

One of the first Bible verses she'd memorized at her grandmother's side.

And one that left her no closer to knowing whether Harrison was a fit father and grandfather for her family.

If the Lord had sent a resounding *No!* from Heaven, or if she'd suddenly heard a Heavenly choir singing a melodious *Yes*—whether they sight-read the music or not—she'd know how to proceed.

But no. That was not the way He worked. Nor had she expected Him to. However, that truth didn't change her situation: Harrison was already in Jase's life and didn't intend to leave. She still needed to know what to do, how to handle Harrison, whether to let him completely into her family's hearts. Maybe Jase was right to watch him for a while first.

Because everything was at stake—her family's happiness, stability and even their safety, as far as their hearts were concerned.

For that reason, this didn't seem like the time to tell Jase who Harrison was. But would waiting hurt Harrison?

Anise raised her gaze and found him watching her, perhaps gauging her emotions, her thoughts, her intentions. She somehow felt comforted that, although his ocean-blues seemed to search her heart through her eyes, they didn't probe, didn't accuse, didn't pass judgment. He seemed simply to wait and prepare to accept and—reassure? Protect?

If she couldn't discern anything else about this situation, she felt confident of two things: she didn't want either Harrison or Jase to be hurt, and Harrison wouldn't reveal his identity to Jase until she was ready.

And she wasn't. More important, her son wasn't ready.

"We can't tell him yet. I'm scared, and—"

He stopped her with a gentle hand on her arm, warmth in his eyes. "We'll wait until you're ready."

And as the late katydids added their harmony to the mockingbird's night song and a chill to her already-uneasy heart, she breathed a desperate, wordless prayer that neither her son nor Harrison would suffer.

Harrison had never thought he'd get into the habit of making house calls, let alone like it. Yet here he was, resisting the urge to grip the arms of his seat late the next afternoon as Anise backed the RV out of Miss Willa Mae's ridiculously narrow drive onto an equally narrow, unpaved road on their way home.

"This is probably the most remote area I've ever seen." He watched the edge of the road, which he might have called a path, and the deep creek beside it and made small talk in an attempt to bridge the distance he sensed between them today. A distance he neither understood nor liked.

"It's remote for me too, and I've lived here nearly all my life," she said, gazing at him and looking pretty as always in her flowered dress, white lab coat and another pair of her high-heeled sandals. "The road is a dead end, six miles long, with Miss Willa Mae's home at the end."

"The only other house I saw on this road was the one about a mile off the highway." But in San Diego, or in any of the other cities he'd lived in during his three years as a travel nurse, no one would have called that two-lane road a highway.

Approaching a sharp curve, Anise slowed the RV to a crawl while Harrison silently prayed for her to keep them out of the creek. The RV got closer to the edge than Harrison was comfortable with, but Anise corrected in time to stay on the road—and stay dry.

"The house you spoke of is around this bend, on the left—the one with the big barn. That's Miss Adah Corbin's farm," she said, her focus locked on the road.

Sure enough, as soon as they'd rounded the bend, he could see the two-story white farmhouse, barn and even a giant gray animal that didn't look exactly like a horse, standing in a pen near the barn. Maybe a mule or a donkey. Not that he would know the difference.

"This is also the closest I've ever been to a barn in my life," he said, hoping to ease Anise's stress and the tension between her brows. "Or that huge animal with the long ears."

It didn't work. "That was Miss Adah's mammoth donkey, Bogey."

He laughed. "Bogey?"

"Miss Adah loves Humphrey Bogart in *The African Queen*."

Naming a donkey after someone you love seemed backward somehow.

"I feel bad asking you to make these after-hours house calls," she said. "But when Miss Willa Mae called and asked me to stop by because her blood pressure was high and her granddaughter's car was broken down, I couldn't tell her no."

"Don't apologize. I wanted to go."

"I wouldn't feel so bad if we hadn't stopped at Colton's house before clinic hours."

She had no clue how wrong she was. Rather than an inconvenience, his time with Colton somehow seemed healing.

He shifted his gaze from the road to Anise, realizing she was way overdue for an explanation of his interest in the boy. "Colton reminds me of my older brother, Martin. He had a diving accident when he was twelve—a year younger than Colton."

With sorrow in her eyes, she glanced at him, looking as if she grieved for Martin.

And knowing her, she did.

"Martin lived three years before he died from pneumonia."

He didn't want to look at her again and see her compassion, since he still sometimes had trouble talking about Martin without getting a little emotional. Which was why he rarely spoke of him.

And yet, something made him want to tell Anise. Maybe it was her tenderness, or her big brown eyes that always held softness, acceptance—love.

"He'd gone to a lake party at a friend's house and tried to do a somersault off the high dive. But he hit the back of his head on the platform and fractured his neck."

Anise's face paled a little as she glanced at him. "Harrison..."

The way she said his name did something to his heart. It was probably the most genuine expression of sympathy he'd ever received for the loss of his big brother.

"Do you have other siblings?"

He shook his head. "No, so Mom counted on me to help give him care."

Harrison met her quick gaze.

"How old were you when you started taking care of him?"

"I was nine when he got hurt. Then my dad started going to the bar after work a lot of nights and coming home after I went to bed. With Dad away so much, I felt driven to take care of Martin, at least, the best I could at that age."

They turned onto the highway, and Anise visibly relaxed on the wider road, which still looked narrow to Harrison. He never thought he'd be so relieved to turn away from a country creek.

"Did you have a good relationship with your father before Martin's accident?"

"I did. In fact, Dad was my flying partner. Every Saturday, he and I went to the airport, and Dad took me up in his beautiful little Skyhawk. He always said that on my twelfth birthday, he'd let me take the controls and fly the plane. But before that happened, Martin passed from pneumonia. His medical bills had mounted up, and Dad had to sell the plane. The buyer took possession on my birthday, and that's also the day Dad left."

"You lost your brother and your father at the same time?" she said, her voice just a whisper.

He nodded. "After I met Lisa in Hawaii and we got married, we moved back to San Diego, where I grew up. Every week for years, I've checked a website that advertises planes for sale in California, looking for the Skyhawk and hoping the owner will put it up for sale someday." Harrison kept his gaze fixed out the window, not wanting to see pity in her face. "There was something special about flying with Dad. I became a flight nurse to try to get that feeling back. All my life, I've just wanted somebody to fly with."

For a moment, Anise said nothing, but he could sense her compassion without words.

"I think someday you'll find someone to fly with."

At the sound of the tenderness in her voice, the old emotion rolled in his throat and chest, as powerful as it had the day Dad left.

As powerful as the day Martin died.

He swallowed back the tightness, the betrayal, the knowledge that Dad didn't want him without Martin. But it simmered just below the surface as always, still making him afraid of the dark places he'd go if he gave in to it.

Time to change the subject.

"We got through it." He drew a deep breath and blew it out, hopefully silently enough that Anise didn't hear. "I've been worried about you today. I get the feeling something's wrong. Do you want to talk about it?"

Her expression unchanged, she merely nodded as if she'd known this moment would come and she'd had no intention of denying or making light of her problem, whatever it was.

Which was refreshing, in a way. Because when was the last time he'd felt secure with a woman and not trapped in some underlying tension, trying to discern truth and figure out what she meant or felt?

"I realize I've been quiet today," she said. "A couple of things have been bothering me. And although they involve you, you didn't cause them."

Harrison took in her now-flushed cheeks as she flipped on the turn signal.

She negotiated the turn and then let out a sigh. "It's embarrassing, and I'm sorry to drag you into this, but when Miss Eugenia sets her mind on something, she hangs on like a dog with a bone."

"What does she want?"

"She asked me—no, she *told* me to borrow Abe's truck, pick up the mums and straw bales from the flower farm and take them to church tonight. Abe can't do it because he barely has time to get to choir practice on time after work."

That was all? But knowing Miss Eugenia, there was more to the story. "What's wrong with that?"

She flipped down the visor, driving against the sun as they hit the Natchez city limits. "I'd have to shift the gears."

His attention darted to the shift knob. Right, this rig was automatic.

He tried to hold back the grin that wanted to break out on his face. "I have a feeling something happened the last time you tried to drive a vehicle with a manual transmission. What was it?"

"A train. Vernon had just left us, and I had a two-hundred-dollar, twenty-year-old car with a four-speed stick shift, which I didn't know how to use. I killed the engine on the slope leading to the railroad track just as a train came barreling toward me. I somehow made it across the tracks and to work, but I walked home after my shift and sold the car the next day."

No wonder she didn't want to drive Abe's truck.

"I've been struggling with this all day, but I couldn't think of a way around it." She pulled into the hospital parking lot and went back to her snail speed as they drove toward the ER entrance.

"Wait, isn't that Jase's Mustang?" Harrison said as they passed the hospital's only clergy parking place. "There can't be many cars like that in a town this size. I hope everybody from the church is okay."

She glanced that way. "That's it, with his corgi bumper sticker. He does hospital visitation on Tuesday afternoons so he can bring any updates on our members to Pastor David before choir practice. The choir has healing prayer for them afterward. But he's always home by now."

"I need to ask you a question, and I'm a little embarrassed about it." She pulled into her spot in the bay, shut off the engine and turned to face Harrison. "Do you know how to drive a stick shift?"

What was so embarrassing about that question? "If you mean a manual transmission, yes."

Anise gave a ladylike little huff, which, combined with her blush, made her seem even cuter than usual. "In that case, I need to ask you to give me a ride in Abe's truck. Miss Eugenia wants me to deliver last night's decorations to the church tonight," she said as she reached beside the seat for her handbag and messenger bag.

They got out, locked the vehicle and strode out of the ER and down the hallway to their offices.

"I've known Miss Eugenia all my life. She always came to our place to buy flowers, shrubs and Christmas trees," Anise said in a near whisper as they passed the radiology department. "Before that, Miss Eugenia's family hired Mamaw as their live-in cook after my grandfather died. Mamaw wanted land to start her flower farm, and Miss Eugenia loaned her the money for a down payment."

"And you inherited the farm."

"So to speak. Since none of my siblings had any kind of relationship with my grandmother, she left the farm, along with the mortgage, to me. But when I could no longer make the payments, it went into foreclosure. Miss Eugenia bought the farm and held it for twelve years until I could buy it back. So, despite her quirkiness, or maybe partly because of it, I've always loved her. And when she asks me to do something, I have a hard time saying no."

"That's why you didn't want to tell her you couldn't deliver the decorations. But doesn't she know you don't drive a manual transmission?"

They arrived at the clinic office, and Anise unlocked the door and stepped in. "She knows everything there is to know about me and my family. In fact, I often wonder if she knows everything about everyone in Natchez."

Harrison followed her and started for his desk. "So she wants me to drive you."

Anise set down her messenger bag and handbag and turned to face him. "In Abe's truck. She told me, 'Have Harrison drive it.' She said it just like that."

He couldn't help the laugh that burst from him. "I've never met anybody like her."

"You won't think the rest of the story is funny." She got up and closed the door, then returned to her desk. "There's an old rumor in

Natchez. It says that, starting back in the late 1950s, a local woman used to pair unmarried ladies with suitable men from all over the South. They call her the famed, mysterious Natchez matchmaker."

"That sounds like something from the nineteenth century, not the twentieth."

"Remember, you're in Natchez, the most traditional, proper city in the South. Even more so than Charleston."

Right. "Who was she?"

"Nobody knows for sure, except the couples she matched, whom she must have sworn to secrecy. But now she has switched from making matches to encouraging romance. In fact, they say she has some sort of instinct about romance, and once she decides a couple is right for each other, she's never failed to see them at the altar. I'm quite sure she had something to do with both my sons' marriages."

All of sudden, he got it. "Is it Miss Eugenia?"

She glanced at the door, eyes wide, and he realized he should have lowered his voice. "Sorry. But…is it?"

"You still don't understand. Yes, I think Miss Eugenia is the mysterious Natchez matchmaker." Anise looked straight at him, leaned forward in her chair toward him. "Harrison, it's only fair for you to know that I'm sure she's trying to match you and me."

He felt his mouth open and then shut. Match them?

Never failed to see them at the altar?

No...

His gaze shot to the tiny office window, and he focused on the white clouds in the blue autumn sky, suddenly wanting to go there.

To escape.

But maybe he wouldn't need to.

Anise looked as appalled as he felt.

They weren't going along with it. He and Anise would stand against Miss Eugenia together.

This time, the matchmaker had met her match.

Chapter Five

The look of horror on Harrison's face would have been funny if it hadn't stung a little.

To his credit, the expression lasted only a split second. It was a relief to know Harrison was no more interested in her than she was in him.

Well, except that she did feel the slightest bit disappointed...

The moment that thought came, she stopped it. It meant nothing. Any woman with eyes—and ears—would find Harrison attractive.

His blue eyes took on a twinkle. "Didn't expect that."

"If you'd known Miss Eugenia as long as I have, it wouldn't have surprised you," she said, leaving behind her mildly hurt feelings and choosing to see the humor instead. "Having never failed to make a match in the past—

which may or may not be true—doesn't mean she never will."

Harrison stood and came near her desk. "I haven't dated since my wife passed. In fact, I'm not sure I've even been alone with a woman since then, other than you this week. I simply don't want another relationship."

"I understand. I don't date either. Since Vernon left, I have said no to every man who has expressed interest." And she always would. Because "yes" was too risky. "I thought you deserved to know her intentions."

His smile came slow, as if he was imagining the future with Miss Eugenia in it. "Thanks for the warning. And yes, I'll drive you and the decorations to the church tonight, as long as Abe doesn't object."

At that moment, Anise realized this man could hold his own, even with the mysterious Natchez matchmaker.

"She's going to do this whether we like it or not, so we might as well decide to enjoy the process," he said, further confirming her thoughts.

"Her meddling doesn't bother me either. I'll live as I sense the Lord asking me, regardless of Miss Eugenia. But remember, she'll throw us together at every opportunity."

"We're already together eight hours a day, so why does she bother?"

The poor, clueless man. "Doing urinalyses and flushing wax out of people's ears isn't romantic. She wants us in romantic situations, like a drive in the country to visit a flower farm."

She caught the comprehension in his eyes.

"Don't worry," he said. "We're onto her, so she can't send any surprises our way."

Harrison crossed the room to his desk and checked his work email while Anise added a few more photographs to the clinic's social media sites. After he'd clocked out on his computer, she locked up the office and they started for the parking lot.

"There's one more thing—and you're free to say no." Outside, Anise stopped at her Jeep, catching sight of Harrison's motorcycle a few spaces down. She turned her gaze to him. "Miss Eugenia has also invited you to join the choir and wants you to come to practice with me tonight."

"Another romantic situation?"

"A pretty church, music, learning together—yes, that would be my guess."

He raised an eyebrow. "That's sneaky, but I'll go along with it."

Anise pushed back a stray lock of hair. "Bring Tiny Romeo over tonight so the dogs can be together while we're gone," she said into the wind.

He jogged to his parking place, straddled the

motorcycle and gave her a two-finger wave as he pulled out of the lot.

She waved back, hoping the two of them could stand their ground against Miss Eugenia without hurting her feelings. Although Anise wished there was a way to spoil her perfect matchmaking record without disappointing her.

Clearly, Anise needed to make this a matter of prayer.

Later, when she let Harrison in the back door, he walked into her kitchen as if he belonged there, even more attractive than this afternoon. Maybe it was because of his cologne. Or it might have been because his long-sleeved, white button-down shirt, cuffed at the wrists, did nothing to conceal his muscular shoulders and arms. It even could have been because he carried Tiny Romeo, who wore a new collar, in one arm and a covered pan of hot ratatouille in the other.

Who knew the man could cook French provincial food?

"I made it this morning," he said, setting Tiny Romeo on the floor and lifting the lid. "I thought you might like to have something ready when you got home tonight, since we don't have much time now."

"This smells great!" Anise breathed in the

aroma of eggplant, peppers, ripe tomatoes, onions and herbs and concluded that the savory dish smelled like home. "How do you know all my favorite foods?"

Sugar skidded into the kitchen and greeted Tiny Romeo with a low, friendly rumble and a sniff to his nose. Then the dogs ran off, their toenails making little clicking sounds on the polished antique pine floor as they chased each other up and down the hall.

Anise locked the dogs inside and drove her Jeep to Armstrong Gym to borrow Abe's truck, Harrison following on his motorcycle. It was ridiculous to drive separately, but she didn't want him to ride with her and thereby fan the flame of Jase's suspicions—or of Miss Eugenia's matchmaking plans. Anise knew well that, in a town the size of Natchez, they could easily run into either the older lady or their son at any street corner between her home and the gym.

Wait—had she just thought of Jase as their son, not her son?

When had that change come to her heart?

She felt a little like a traitor—but who was she betraying? Vernon? No, because even before he'd abandoned them, he'd never been a true father to either boy, especially Jase.

Maybe the thought had betrayed Jase a little, since he didn't yet know he had a father.

Certainly not Abe. As much as he liked Harrison, he'd consider it a win, not a loss.

That left only Anise—a traitor to no one but herself as she acknowledged the fact that, when the time came for her and Harrison's big reveal, she'd no longer be Jase's only parent. For the rest of her life, she'd have to share her younger son with Harrison. And while she admitted he'd probably be a great father to Jase, she knew sharing him would be hard, in a way.

As she pulled into the Armstrong Gym parking lot, she breathed a quick prayer for them—all three of them. And for her and Harrison to escape whatever romantic situation Miss Eugenia had cooked up.

She got out and hurried into the gym, where she waited for Abe to remove the truck's key fob from his giant ring of house, gym and church keys. When she'd returned to the parking lot and had settled into the truck's passenger side, Harrison started the engine and headed for Mockingbird Creek.

He glanced at his watch. "Can we make it to the church in time for choir practice?"

"It'll be close."

Hand on the gear shift, he moved the handle without seeming to give it thought, as if by instinct.

When she and Harrison took off for the

flower farm, something else rankled inside Anise. She was a grown woman—a mother and grandmother—who'd had to ask someone to drive her, like a girl who wanted to go to the mall. Why had she given up on learning to drive that old jalopy back then? She'd kept her family together against all odds, started paying Vernon's debts a few dollars at a time on nurse's aide pay, graduated from college and was now debt-free and ran a clinic.

Surely she could learn to shift a car.

Each time Harrison changed gears, her determination grew until it became a challenge she had to meet. She'd either have to learn to drive Abe's truck or live with regret.

She had enough of that in her life already.

Harrison downshifted as they approached the flower farm. She watched his motions closely. One hand on the wheel, the other moving the gearshift, feet pressing and depressing the accelerator, clutch and brake—Harrison's actions flowed as gracefully as a ballroom dance.

She didn't know how to waltz, but she could do this. She just knew it.

But Joseph had fallen yesterday. At his age, he'd probably be sore for a while, so she couldn't ask him to teach her. Neither could she ask her sons. They remembered the train incident, and she wasn't interested in listening to their objections and seeing fear in their eyes. And she sure didn't want to hear them say they thought she couldn't or shouldn't do it.

"Harrison," she said, before she could lose her courage, "would you teach me how to shift?"

His eyes flew open wide, then they turned mischievous. "I'll teach you. But you'd better make sure Abe is willing to take the chance with his truck. And stay away from railroad tracks."

His good-natured ribbing made her laugh.

This was going to work out just fine.

They quickly loaded the mums, pumpkins, and straw bales onto the truck bed, drove back to town and pulled in at church with minutes to spare before practice. With the parking lot full and the church lights on, Harrison lowered the tailgate under the canopy, the light evening breeze cooling Anise even as it swirled the longer top of Harrison's dark military-style fade into adorable disarray.

Anise couldn't help smiling.

As Harrison hefted straw bales from the truck bed and stacked them beside the door, Anise carried the pumpkins and mums inside. Then, while he parked the truck, she scanned the parking lot for Jase's car.

Jase should have been here by now. He never failed to come early on choir night. Surely nothing was wrong with Erin or Bella...

Then she remembered seeing his car in the hospital clergy parking space. That meant something was probably wrong with someone in their church or community, not with his family. She stopped to pray silently for that person, whoever he or she was.

Harrison jogged back to the canopy and held the door for her. Entering the foyer, they found the whole choir there, chatting and holding their light jackets and purses.

Why had they congregated here in the foyer instead of the choir room?

"Something's not right," Anise said, taking a step toward the crowd.

"Mama, can you take Bella?"

At the sound of Jase's voice behind her, she turned to face him, his voice sounding more like Harrison's than ever.

Her son must have come in through the hallway to his office. He held sleeping Bella, his diaper backpack slung over one shoulder.

She saw the moment he caught sight of Harrison. Something changed in his eyes, and instead of handing Bella to her, he pulled his daughter closer as if afraid someone might steal her away.

And it hit her.

Her son wasn't afraid Harrison would hurt only Anise or himself.

Jase feared Harrison would steal Bella's heart,

and maybe the new babies' too, in time—and would then disappear.

Just as Vernon had.

Her hand flew to her mouth as she remembered that Bella's biological grandmother had tried to snatch the then newborn girl from them—here at this church.

Vernon had left them without a word the afternoon he was supposed to have picked up Jase from a Sunday school event, leaving Jase all alone—here at this church.

And now Harrison, the biggest threat in Jase's life, showed up with Anise.

Here at this church.

A hush as heavy as the straw bales had fallen over the room at the sound of Jase's voice. She spun to face the choir and caught sight of their surprised expressions.

Turning back to Jase, she noticed it.

His hair.

He'd had it cut, almost exactly like Harrison's. Looking at them, Anise saw the same longish, dark military-style fade, the same stunning blue eyes, the same muscular build. Even similar white shirts with cuffed-up sleeves.

She felt the blood drain from her face. Everyone in this room could surely see the resemblance as the two men stood side by side. Soon the whole town would know—

"Let's get this rehearsal started," a strident voice called from the back of the foyer. "We're already ten minutes late. If we don't get moving, I'm going to miss the opening of *Jeopardy!*"

Eldeen Rogers, the town gossip. At least she wasn't close enough to see what was happening here at the door.

"What's going on?" The foyer door had opened again, and Pastor David strode in, his gait steady and his voice strong—no doubt a result of his Rock Steady Boxing classes, which helped control some of his Parkinson's symptoms.

"Nobody was here to unlock the choir room," Eldeen said in that raucous tone of hers.

Pastor David turned to Jase, concern in his eyes, then he focused on the toddler in his arms. "Is Erin all right? You don't usually bring Bella to choir practice."

"She's worn out tonight, so I brought Bella," Jase said, keeping his gaze averted from Harrison as if the man would go away if Jase ignored him. "I'm sorry to be late, but I stayed longer at the hospital because Joseph Duncan was admitted. The pain in his ankle got worse overnight, and Miss Eugenia finally convinced him to go. It's broken. He wanted me to tell y'all and to ask for your prayers."

Which explained why Jase's car was at the hospital later than usual.

But he must have come in the foyer right behind Anise and Harrison, so why hadn't they seen or heard him?

Then Miss Eugenia came out of the hallway to Jase's office, wearing an innocent look on her face.

A phony innocent look. Anise knew it well.

They must have parked in the side parking lot and come in through the hallway door between Pastor David's office and Jase's. But what had Miss Eugenia been doing in there, and why was she trying to cover it up?

"We'd better get practice started, Jase," Pastor David said as he pulled his keys from his pocket, his gaze shifting from Harrison to Jase and back, and then to Anise. "Good to see you again, Harrison."

As the pastor started toward the choir room, the crowd parted to make way for him.

"Jase, I can take Bella for you," Anise said.

"That's okay, Mama. I'll keep her."

She had a feeling he might have wanted to say *I'll keep her safe*.

Anise glanced over at Harrison, who merely stood back and waited, probably to ease the situation or at least keep from adding to the tension.

Naturally, Miss Eugenia slipped through the crowd and followed directly behind Jase, beckoning Miss Eldeen to come with her. Good.

With those two leading the way, the rest would follow. Maybe then they could get this practice over with and get out of here.

"Zeke, you remember Harrison Mitchell from last Sunday," Miss Eugenia said to the piano player, who had recently become choir director and worship leader.

He looked Harrison over as if sizing him up, then he offered his hand. "Sure. Bass, right?"

"That's right," Harrison said, his brows raised.

Apparently, Miss Eugenia had already informed Zeke what part Harrison sang.

"Basses are over there by the robe closet." Zeke handed him a folder with sheet music, giving him a sidewise glance Anise had seen before. Having lived the hard life of a back-street-bar musician, in trouble with the law more than once before he'd given his life to Jesus five or so years ago, Zeke seemed to pick up on certain things fast. "Stand next to Jase."

Anise should have seen that coming.

Harrison hesitated.

Jase turned to Anise and handed sleeping Bella to her as if he didn't want his daughter near Harrison. Anise lifted the toddler to her shoulder and held her tight, every breath a prayer for the father and son.

Harrison inched his way to Jase's side. He

gave her son—his son—a warm smile that had to have been laced with pain, since he surely knew Jase would reject his friendly effort.

"Everybody open 'Be Thou My Vision.' This is a new arrangement for our Homecoming service. Harrison, are you familiar with Homecoming?"

"I assume you're not talking about football, so no," Harrison said.

"It's an old country church thing, on the same Sunday each year, always in the fall. We have lots of visitors, including former members who have moved away or now belong to other churches, our district officers, and the community in general. We have lots of music, a special speaker and dinner on the grounds."

"Dinner on the grounds is just an old-fashioned way of saying we eat outside. We make fried chicken and all the fixings before church," someone behind him said in a stage whisper.

He turned around. It was Miss Eugenia.

"So we want to get the music right," Zeke went on. "Basses and tenors start, and the women come in at measure thirty-five."

From her place with the sopranos on the other side of the room, Bella still asleep in her arms, Anise kept one eye on her music and the other on the two men.

Zeke played through the introduction, directing from the piano. He lifted his left hand at measure five, signaling the tenors and basses to come in. Two identical, powerful bass voices responded, soaring above the others, smooth as gourmet chocolate and twice as rich.

Anise's hand trembled, her sheet music shaking as if a cold creek wind blew through the room.

One voice drifted off, she couldn't tell which, leaving the other to continue alone for a moment then stop.

Jase turned to Harrison, his mouth gaping. Clearly, he'd recognized their twin voices. The rest of the choir dropped out as well, probably sensing something was very wrong.

Closing his mouth, Jase faced the front again, his gaze boring straight ahead into the mirror in front of them, the one they'd used to check their choir robes, back in the days when they wore them.

Anise shot a glance at the mirror, the palpable tension tying a knot in her middle.

All at once, just as she'd feared, Jase's gaze bounded from his own image to Harrison's and back.

Same eyes, same hair. Same voice. Even the same shirt.

She saw the moment realization swept through her son. But instead of the anger or pain she'd have expected, she saw fear mixed with—confusion.

For all the world, he looked like the little boy who hadn't understood why his father never came to the church that day to pick him up. And why he had never come back.

Oh, Lord, it was easier when he just kept a distance from Harrison...

Then she realized that the accompaniment had stopped.

Zeke looked over the top of the console piano, a question in his face. "What happened? Y'all were sounding great—"

"I'd better go home and check on Erin. Mama, I'll take Bella."

Jase headed for Anise, who stood between him and the door, pitching his folder on top of the piano as he passed it.

"Pastor Jase, hold on." Zeke shoved back his piano bench and bounded out from behind the instrument, following Jase. "What's going on?"

Jase held out his hands for Bella, but Anise shifted, keeping her hold on her granddaughter. "You can't run out like this, Jase. You have to think of Bella."

Her son visibly swallowed—hard—clearly trying to maintain his composure in front of this flock the Lord had called him to help shepherd.

"Believe me," his quiet voice dropped an octave, "I'm thinking of Bella."

"Jase, no..." She kept her voice so low, she wasn't sure he heard.

"Please give me my daughter, Mama."

She tried to untangle Bella's arms from her neck, but she awakened, letting out a whimper and clinging tighter to her grandmother. Anise grabbed her handbag instead and started out the door, still holding the little girl close. In the hallway, she turned to see both Jase and Harrison following her.

Jase reached for Bella but, still sleepy, she snuggled into her grandmother's neck and clung to her all the harder. When he tried to pull her away, the girl started to cry.

"Mama, I just can't..."

His jaw tightening and his breaths suddenly jagged, Jase gave up and turned away, his posture bent like that of an old man, his hand covering his eyes.

She touched his arm, his back still to her, and breathed a wordless prayer. Nothing had prepared her for this level of pain in her son. Not Vernon's betrayal, not his two broken engagements—not even the time he'd thought Erin would move to Japan instead of staying here and becoming engaged to him.

"He's my birth father, isn't he?" he said, turning to her, a jagged edge to his voice.

She nodded.

The expression in her son's beautiful eyes wrecked her. *Lord, You have to fix this. I don't know what to do.*

At that moment, the only thing she did know was that their family would never again be the same.

Jase's animosity toward Harrison hung in the air like fog in the San Francisco Bay—thick, immovable and dangerous.

Before Harrison came to Natchez, he hadn't necessarily expected his son to jump for joy when he found him. In fact, he'd thought he'd prepared himself for the worst. But now, as he heard Anise and Jase exchanging tension-filled words outside the choir room, Harrison remembered the do-or-die tone in Anise's voice last night. She'd probably thought he hadn't noticed the way Jase scowled at him while he played drop-and-roll tag with Georgia. But he couldn't have missed it if he'd tried.

He had to believe this turn of events was from the Lord. Since neither Harrison nor Anise had known how to handle their situation, and they had asked Him to intervene, the only logical conclusion was that He had done so.

And now that the truth was out, Harrison hardly knew whether to breathe a sigh of relief or gulp a lungful of air in panic.

At the moment, he leaned toward panic.

Who'd have thought Jase would cut his hair almost exactly like Harrison's? Had that been a coincidence, or had Jase already subconsciously realized who Harrison was and wanted a father he could imitate and in whose footsteps he could follow? Regardless, there was no doubt Jase knew who he was. Also no doubt that he wasn't happy with the knowledge.

He'd been right that revealing his identity to Jase could hurt him. In a way, Harrison had begun to dread the day his son would learn he hadn't cared enough about Starr to treat her as a real man should. He'd been angry with himself for that ever since the letter came from the attorney.

Now he had to stand back and watch his son learn what kind of man Harrison had been back then.

That scared him more than the first time he did CPR.

He heard the sound of footsteps approaching from behind him, and within seconds, Anise laid her hand on his upper arm. "Let's go in the sanctuary," she said, heading in that direction without waiting for either Harrison or Jase to object.

They strode up the aisle behind her. She laid Bella on the front pew, careful not to wake her, and gestured for the men to sit on either side of her.

The dim light, shining through the glass in the sanctuary doors, made the room feel foreboding. Harrison picked up a leftover bulletin from the seat and sat in the pew, a good three feet from Anise, and crossed one ankle over his knee.

"Harrison, I don't know why you're here or what you want from me, but it's pretty clear who you are." Jase's voice held a ragged edge, deeper than usual and his Southern accent more pronounced. "Because there's no denying I'm the twenty-five-year-younger version of you."

Twenty-three, actually.

Maybe this was why Trevor had warned Harrison that his son might not be thrilled to have his long-lost father show up unexpectedly. Had he been wrong? Should he have asked the lawyer to find Jase instead of coming here himself, or maybe to call his son and ask if he wanted to meet Harrison?

No point in trying to figure it out now. It was done, Harrison was here, and his son clearly wanted him to leave.

Maybe he should.

Because the family he desperately wanted didn't want him.

Bella stirred then, her dark hair damp after her nap, her big blue eyes half-open as she reached for Anise. "Nannie…"

Anise picked her up and rocked her gently in her seat, stirring an ache in his heart. Her slow rhythm seemed infused with grace. With love. And acceptance.

Qualities Harrison had longed for since Lisa passed. Actually, since the first few years of their marriage, or even since long before that.

Maybe he hadn't felt completely loved since Martin got hurt.

As far as his marriage was concerned, it was probably Harrison's fault, since he hadn't been able to make Lisa happy since her forty-first birthday. She'd held on to hope for a child through her fortieth year. But that next birthday, she'd faced the facts and given up on becoming a mother.

That day, their marriage officially died.

Until this moment, he hadn't realized how much he wanted a family, a home. Specifically, he wanted to be a part of Jase's Natchez family and have a real home here. One where relatives stopped by unexpectedly, where he entertained them, where he could give of himself and show love.

Most of all, a home where he could be a father to Jase and a grandpa to Bella and the unborn twins.

But none of that would happen if he couldn't somehow get on Jase's good side.

Harrison drew a deep breath and realized his next words could be some of the most important he'd ever spoken. He paused and silently asked the Lord to direct his mouth. Then he prayed for an extra measure of grace because, without it, there was no way any of them would come out of this room unhurt.

"Jase," he said, lowering his voice to what he hoped was a gentle tone and uncrossing his legs to keep his posture neutral, "two weeks before I came to Natchez, I got a letter from an attorney in Nashville."

He reached for his wallet, pulled out the tattered paper and handed it to Jase.

Jase accepted the page, hesitated a moment and then read.

The seconds passed like hours until Jase finally looked up. "So the woman named in this letter is my birth mother."

"She is, Jase," Anise said. "Your father and I knew her during our Nashville days."

"Did you know Harrison back then?"

"We knew of him," she said, seeming to take care in choosing her words, "but we never met."

"But if you and Starr were such good friends that she gave me to you, why didn't you ever meet Harrison?"

Anise turned to Harrison, silent, letting him know she thought it was his responsibility to answer this one. And she was right.

Lord, help me here. "In those days, I wasn't the kind of man you are. I graduated from nursing school, worked a year in a local hospital and then got a job as a travel nurse. My only objectives were to see as much of the world as I could and to have a good time."

"So my birth mother was just a girl you had fun with, not one you were in love with."

Yeah, that was pretty close to the truth.

The guilt he still felt was well deserved, considering the way he'd treated her. Sure, he'd been young and ignorant and full of himself. But that was no excuse for having a casual relationship with Starr, never intending to marry her. What had he been thinking, anyway?

"Jase, I wasn't raised in church like you were. A friend's family picked me up for services from time to time, and I learned a little Bible and prayed some, especially after my brother's accident. But I didn't know the Lord at all until I was married. After that, my heart and life changed. But yes. I lived a reckless, selfish life in Nashville."

Harrison couldn't tell if Jase's silence was a good sign or a bad one.

Finally, Jase looked up. "What does your wife think about this?"

"She passed away five years ago, so she never knew about you." He was just glad the lawyer's letter hadn't come while Lisa was still alive. He wasn't sure their marriage would have survived her knowing he had a child.

And now, Harrison's long-ago girlfriend had torn out his heart while giving him hope of a future family.

"Harrison, are you all right?"

He turned toward Anise's kind voice. The concern in her eyes brought him back to the moment—a relief, really.

"I'm fine. But shame has a way of sneaking up on you and dragging you down when you don't expect it." Needing a distraction, he glanced at the Bible Verse of the Week section at the end of last Sunday's bulletin he still held. Psalm 120:1: *In my distress I cried unto the Lord, and he heard me.*

That was good news, since clearly all three of them were in distress, and he was sure all three of them had also cried out to the Lord about this situation. So surely He'd heard them.

"I don't know where we should start," Jase said. "Why did you come here, Harrison? And why all the sneaking around? You could have called me from California, or you could have come right out and told me who you were."

Now that he had to explain his reasons to Jase, they seemed flimsy. "I didn't know your name, and neither did the lawyer. My internet searches didn't turn up anyone named Annie Barrett Browning. The attorney's letter was based on information Starr gave a nurse on her deathbed. So I came to find you, to discover what kind of man you were, and then I planned to reveal my identity at the right time."

"Harrison and I talked this through numerous times," Anise said. "For your sake, we decided together to wait for the right time to tell you that Harrison is your father."

Jase drew in a breath, let it out slowly. "You knew all along and kept it from me, Mama?"

"It was for the best," she said in what might have been her mom voice when her sons were young. "You said you didn't like Harrison. You never stopped scowling when he was around— you were rude to him. But you had no basis for not liking him."

"I also said I didn't like him because he was after you." He turned to Harrison. "Look, I don't have anything against you as a guy. But I can see what's happening between you and my mother. You two have enough chemistry going on to make your own romance movie, but you both keep denying it."

Anise puffed out a breath. "Jase, that is simply not true."

Chemistry? What exactly did Jase think he was seeing between them? Sure, Anise was cute, especially tonight in her flared jeans, ruffle-sleeved light blue shirt and brown sandals with about three-inch heels. She was smart and kind and intuitive, and she was a great mother and grandmother, but he sure wasn't in love with her. He couldn't risk that, after the mess he'd made of his marriage.

But he had to admit, if he was looking for a girlfriend—or whatever you call that at their age—she'd be his first choice.

He watched a frown form between Anise's eyes. "You're the only person who thinks that, Jase. Besides, what if I wanted to date? My husband is dead, and I could have a relationship with a man if I wanted to. I'm even free to marry again."

"I have to side with your mother on that, Jase," Harrison said. "She's a grown woman and can make her own decisions."

Jase turned to Anise, lowering his voice. "I'm just scared that you might make a mistake. After Dad left, you became everything to me and Abe, and you still are, other than our own families.

You gave up having any kind of life of your own, because when you weren't working, you took care of us and tried to fix up our old shack and make it a home. You did whatever it took to keep us together—"

He stopped, his voice cracking. Swallowed hard. "I was awake the night Miss Eugenia came over, about a week before Christmas, just a couple months after Dad abandoned us. I lay in my bed and heard Miss Eugenia talk about all the debt Dad left you with, and the condition of the falling-down house the banker gave you after he foreclosed on the house you and Dad bought. I heard her say you couldn't make enough money to keep both of us."

Anise swiped a tear from her cheek. The depth of love and warmth in her eyes, shimmering in the soft light, ignited a long-dormant ache in Harrison's heart.

"And then I heard her offer to take me," Jase said, showing no indication that love like his mother had shown him was anything but an everyday experience.

Then a new thought burst into Harrison's mind and somehow ripped into his heart as well—what if Jase really did feel this kind of love from his mother every day?

What if Harrison could one day feel love, give love, like that?

A cynical laugh nearly escaped his lips at the thought. No one as broken as Harrison could give that kind of love. And no one as broken as Harrison deserved to receive it. His marriage taught him that.

"She said she'd take me as a foster child, or that she'd adopt me," Jase went on, oblivious to the pain and confusion raging inside Harrison.

"That was the worst day of my life," she said, her voice as soft as her eyes. "I told her no, of course. I never could have given you to anyone."

"Other mothers have. But do you remember what you told her? You said I'd been given away once, and you weren't going to let me be given away again."

"I meant every word," Anise said. "But I admit there were days when I questioned my decision. Days when we had no groceries in the house. Then the Lord would send someone with money or food. And days when I had to drop you off at school in your classmates' hand-me-downs. After you and Abe were asleep at night, I'd go into your room and watch you sleep, trusting me to take care of you, and then I'd realize keeping you was the right thing."

"But, see, Mama? Ever since Dad left, it's been you and me and Abe against the world. If you'd handed me over to Miss Eugenia, you wouldn't have had to work so hard. But you didn't. You took care of us, and I want to make sure you're taken care of too."

"You're right—we did fight to stay together. And I appreciate you wanting to protect me. But I have enough life experience to know what I'm doing. And now I'm asking you to give Harrison a chance. He's your father, and he can be a help to you and the children. You might be able to add something to his life too. Like love and acceptance." Anise shifted Bella to her other arm, causing the little girl to stir and look at Harrison with those big blue eyes.

A blue so close to Harrison and Jase's that a stranger might think she was related to them by blood.

Would Jase do it? Would he give Harrison a chance to prove that all he wanted was to be there for this new family of his?

Jase gazed down at his daughter for so long, Harrison began to fear his son might refuse Anise's request, even ask him to leave town. Then Jase touched Bella's hair, spread over Anise's arm. "Bella was an orphan, Harrison. I won't let her be alone again. So if you want a place in her life, I need your promise that you'll continue to be a grandfather to her for the rest of your life. And to our twins and to any other children we might have."

Starting to feel a little wrung out, and realizing he'd been holding his breath, Harrison exhaled with a puff.

Thank You, Lord.

He'd never been more sure of a promise than this one. "You have my word."

"And I want proof that you're really my father."

"I ordered paternity test kits as soon as I got to town," Harrison said. "The clinic has been cancelled tomorrow because there's a funeral at the church where we were to hold it, and they don't want us to disrupt things. Can you meet me at my house at eight? I'll make breakfast, and then we can take the test."

"Sure. But, Harrison, please try to remember how new this is to me. And that I've never had a good father. I assume you came here to build a relationship with me." Jase kept his voice low. "But to be honest, how do I know that? I don't have much money, but the thought that you might be after something still crosses my mind. That makes it difficult for me to take you into our family."

"Then take him by faith, Jase." Anise's soft voice stilled the tension in the atmosphere and brought a sense of stability, of calmness.

A calmness that extended to Harrison's jangled nerves and helped him understand Jase's fears. His son didn't dislike him. He simply didn't want his mother or his child hurt.

And since Harrison had no romantic intentions toward Anise, that part would work out fine.

"Jase, I assure you that nothing is going on between your mother and me, except our jobs and our concern for you," he said. "I just want to get to know you and your family more and hopefully be of some help to you someday. Can you trust me on this?"

Jase hesitated so long, Harrison started to fear his answer.

Finally he nodded, stood and took little Bella from Anise. "I don't want to. But I'm going to trust you…by faith."

And at that moment, trust was enough.

Chapter Six

The warmth of the Natchez September afternoon had given way to a cool evening when Anise, Jase and Harrison left the sanctuary. But something niggled at the back of her mind, not letting her completely relish Jase's apparent change of heart. Or the recent break from summer's ferocious heat.

No matter how hard she tried, she couldn't remember what she'd seen or heard that triggered the sense of mystery she couldn't shake.

Dark and quiet, the church looked and felt empty. Apparently, choir practice had ended early, and everyone had gone home.

Then she heard light, quick footsteps coming from the direction of the choir room.

"Jase, are you ready?" Sure enough, Miss Eugenia headed toward them as if on a mission.

Right. Jase had brought her to practice. She

must have gone to the hospital with him. Or he might have picked her up at home, since Abe hadn't come tonight. She couldn't drive her golf cart to church as she did in the summer, with dusk falling earlier now.

"We're ready. I'll bring the car to the canopy and pick you up." He shifted Bella to his left arm and stuck his right hand into his pants pocket, presumably for his keys.

A funny look crossed his face. He headed for his office. "I must have left the keys on my desk when I stopped to get the Homecoming Sunday schedule for you, Miss Eugenia."

On his desk...

That was it.

Miss Eugenia and Jase had come in through the side door, into the hallway where Jase and Pastor David had their offices. But Jase had come right in, while Miss Eugenia lagged behind and appeared in the foyer later.

Why had she lingered in the hallway? It contained only the two offices.

Within moments, Jase was back. "My office door's locked. I have no idea how that happened."

Well, Anise did. She shot Miss Eugenia a glance. The older lady just smiled that tight little smile she used when she was either up to something or meant to get her way.

She'd locked that door, all right. She must

have seen her chance to push the button on the doorknob and pull the door shut when Jase left the room with his keys inside. But why?

"Who else is still here, Miss Eugenia?" Jase asked.

She held out her hands as if indicating that the whole choir had slipped through her fingers. "They've all gone home. Zeke didn't want to continue without Jase's strong voice. The other basses can't hit the right notes if Jase isn't there for them to follow. Besides, Eldeen kept complaining about the time. You know how her whole world revolves around watching *Jeopardy!*"

"Pastor David left too?" A frown flitted across Jase's face.

"He went to the hospital to see Joseph Duncan," Miss Eugenia said, a little telltale lilt in her voice.

Anise could imagine who'd encouraged him to go. She glanced at Harrison, who stood behind Miss Eugenia and shrugged. She quietly stepped over to him, hoping not to draw attention. "Miss Eugenia is up to something," she whispered.

"That's what I thought too." Harrison's eyes twinkled as he whispered back. He poured himself a cup of coffee from the foyer's refreshment station, added sugar and stirred. Then he turned off the pot and took a sip. "Jase seems oblivious."

"He thinks she can do no wrong." Even though he'd suspected Miss Eugenia of match-making when Erin first came to Natchez.

Jase pulled out his phone. "I'll have to call one of the deacons to come and unlock the secretary's office so I can get the spare keys from the safe. Joseph is obviously out, so that leaves Abe and Zeke."

"Zeke is on his way to Vidalia on his motorcycle, so he won't answer," Miss Eugenia said.

"Guess Abe's the man, then." He stepped away to place the call.

Miss Eugenia joined Anise and Harrison by the door. "Harrison, the little we heard from you tonight sounded wonderful. Zeke said he definitely wants you in the choir. Maybe he'll even give you a solo. Or a duet with Jase. Wouldn't that be nice?"

The way she said it, it sounded as if the older lady had figured out who Harrison was. How did she always seem to know—

"Abe had to go back to the gym. The security alarm went off." Jase pocketed his phone. "The police think it was a malfunction, but they're going to be there for a while."

"Maybe Anise should check your office door again, Jase," Miss Eugenia said.

He shook his head. "Believe me, it's locked."

"Try anyway, Anise."

Her tone told Anise that she wouldn't abide an argument, so she strode through the hallway to her son's office and rattled the doorknob. Sure enough, it was locked.

"We all need to get home, especially Bella," Anise called into the foyer. Then she ambled to the hallway door and tried the handle. It was locked too. "The five of us won't fit in Abe's truck. It holds only two in the back seat, since it just has those little flip-up seats."

She peered out the door glass, searching her mind for a solution. Then she noticed something didn't look right with Jase's car.

The front passenger window was rolled down about three inches.

This was getting strange. An office door that was supposed to be unlocked was locked, and the window Jase always kept closed was open.

Anise headed toward the foyer again and told Jase about the window.

"I'll go out and close it in a minute. I promised Miss Fannie that I'd always keep the windows closed when I park the car."

"The Mustang Jase drives belonged to Miss Fannie's late husband, Colonel Chester," Anise told Harrison.

The Mustang and Miss Fannie made Anise

think of the "coincidences" that had thrown Jase and Erin together a year ago. How much had Miss Eugenia had to do with that, back when Erin was Miss Fannie's private nurse?

"Why don't you two walk down to the river?" Miss Eugenia said, interrupting Anise's thoughts as if she could read her mind. "It's a beautiful evening, and you can show Harrison the bluff. Have you seen our river yet?"

"The Mississippi River, right?" Harrison asked with just the right amount of respect in his tone for both Miss Eugenia and their mighty river and with none of the frustration Anise currently felt with the older lady. "I once saw it from the Stone Arch Bridge in Minneapolis."

She shook her head. "You haven't seen the Mississippi River until you've seen it from the Natchez bluff. Anise, why don't you show Harrison the bluff trail and the Bridge of Sighs? From there, it's an easy walk to the gym, where you can pick up your vehicles. That way Jase, Bella and I can go home in Abe's truck."

Was that what this was about? Getting Anise and Harrison to take an evening walk by the river? She opened her mouth to protest. But if she refused to walk with him, they'd all have to stay until Abe could get there with his van. And none of them knew how long that would take.

She had no good reason not to go, except for being weary of Miss Eugenia's matchmaking.

"Bridge of Sighs, like the one in Venice?" Harrison asked.

"It's a pedestrian bridge with a great view of the river. The original bridge, built in the nineteenth century, was named after the Venice bridge," Anise said. "I'm not sure they knew Venice's Bridge of Sighs was not remotely sentimental in those days, except for the convicts sighing as they looked through the bridge's windows to get their last glimpse of their city. The original Bridge of Sighs connected the palace with the prison."

Miss Eugenia gave a ladylike sniff. "In Venice, yes, long ago. But our bridge is quite romantic."

"Romantic or not, I need to get this child home." Jase handed Bella to Anise and headed for the door. "Since the window's open in the car, I can get a hanger from the coat rack, unlock the door, and get her car seat. Besides the cool factor, this is a major advantage to having an old Mustang."

"Anise, what do you think?" Harrison drained his cup and threw it away. "Are you up for walking? I wouldn't mind seeing the river."

She hesitated, but only for a moment. Whatever else happened, she didn't intend to live in fear of one of Miss Eugenia's schemes. "Sure. The sunset's beautiful over the river. I often walk or take a run to the park at dusk."

Jase came back in, having left Bella's car seat outside, and Anise handed the toddler to him. As she left, she caught a glimpse of Miss Eugenia out of the corner of her eye.

The older woman gave her a saucy wave as if she knew Anise was on to her. Did that mean she wasn't trying to hide her matchmaking efforts? With Miss Eugenia, one never knew what to expect.

Anise and Harrison started toward Broadway, their pace slow as if neither wanted to broach the subject that hovered between them like the patchy clouds overhead. Despite Miss Eugenia's insistence that it was a beautiful night, it seemed as if those clouds hadn't yet decided whether to hold their peace or pour down a deluge.

"I hope we won't get wet," Harrison said, gazing up at the sky.

"Yes, but the clouds will make the sunset spectacular."

"Funny how that works."

Was he talking about the weather or their lives? Anise couldn't be sure.

"It's good to have it out in the open with Jase now, although I wish we'd had the conversation in private," Harrison said. "I didn't stop to think that Zeke would have me stand next to Jase."

"I'm amazed how much you sound alike. I'm sure that tipped Jase off. But you couldn't have known your voices are nearly identical."

"I did know, because I heard him sing at your house. But it would have seemed strange to come to choir practice and not sing."

That made sense.

"I'm guessing Abe is in the choir too, having inherited your vocal genes."

She nodded. "Vernon's too. That man could do an Elvis impression that would make you think the King of Rock and Roll was at the mic."

"Vernon sang rock in Nashville?"

"Just for side gigs, when somebody wanted an Elvis impersonator. His first love was country music."

They turned onto Main Street and headed for Roth's Hill Road and the bridge. "Sounds like your husband got to live his dreams."

"He wanted to be as big as Elvis, and he had the talent to do it." How long had it been since she'd given more than a moment's thought to those days? So long that they seemed almost like something she'd read in a book or seen in a movie, not real life. "But you don't live the Nashville music scene long before you learn how much talent is waiting tables in seedy bars and all-night diners."

Like Starr.

"What happened to Vernon's dream?" he asked.

They started up the ramp leading to the Bridge of Sighs, and Anise let out a sigh of her own. "After I got pregnant with Abe, I wanted to come home. I'd had enough of the night life and the insecurity of living on the small wages we earned in our occasional small-time gigs and my waitressing job."

"From the look on your face, I'd say you're leaving something out."

How perceptive. "Vernon and I started having marriage problems when a major record label offered me—not him—a contract, and I turned it down."

Harrison stopped in the middle of the ramp. "You had a chance to be a star."

A star. How many times had she heard Vernon throw that word around? Except he almost always used it in reference to himself, not her. "It was still a long shot. Even with a label as big as that one, not every artist makes it. I guess we'll never know."

"So Vernon didn't want you to have the contract instead of him, but he didn't want you to turn it down either."

"Right. But I was pregnant then and realized I didn't want to raise my child in the kind of life we had. It wasn't long before his jealousy and spitefulness drove a wedge between us. When Abe was a year old, I insisted on going home. That's when Starr asked me to take Jase with us."

They stepped onto the pedestrian bridge that spanned the two-hundred-foot-high bluffs and caught sight of the river. The sky a fiery red, the river reflected the glow under the Natchez-Vidalia bridge in the distance.

"Miss Eugenia was right about the view," Harrison said as he rested his arms on the Bridge of Sighs railing and took in the sunset for a moment before turning to her. "If becoming a star was Vernon's dream, what was yours?"

That was easy. "Remember, I was only seventeen. My dream was to leave Mockingbird Creek."

"What about now?" Those blue eyes bore into hers and wouldn't stop. "What's your dream?"

"Making the clinic succeed."

He laughed. "You did that the first day. What else?"

Anise had to think about that. "My safe place was always with Mamaw. And my happy place was the flower farm."

"Good. What are you going to do with it?"

In her mind, Anise swept her gaze over the property, its shabby fields, unkempt yard, and dilapidated bait shop. She should have done something with Mamaw's farm years ago. The whole place looked as if no one cared.

Mamaw would cry if she could see it now.

Except for the bait shop. Seeing it empty and falling down would probably make her grandmother happy, since she'd hated it as much as Anise did. In fact, Mamaw would be happier yet if it did fall down.

But what more could Anise do than pay the taxes, have the yard mowed a couple times a month and tamp down her regret every time she imagined her grandmother's bent back as she tended the flowers she loved? Mamaw had chosen her career, and Anise had chosen hers. She could hardly leave the clinic behind and start over as a farmer.

Even as a flower farmer.

She turned from Harrison and looked out across the water to the Louisiana side of the river. "I guess I'll do the same thing with it that I've done all these years."

"What would you do with the farm if you could make it anything you want?"

She didn't have to think about that. "I'd hire someone to pull all the weeds in the fields so the perennials could grow the way they used to."

He set his hands on his hips and looked out across the river as if he'd lived here all his life, as if he knew its every bend, silt bar and current. As if silently encouraging her to dream big. Mississippi River big. "Then what?"

Seeing him on that bridge, one elbow leaning against it, his stance confident and casual, Anise had to wonder how was it that, everywhere this man went, he blended right in as if he'd always belonged there? Like right now, when he looked as comfortable as he had in the clinic, the gym and the church. He'd carried that sense of confidence into church tonight and stepped right into a position in the choir. Did he just go around feeling like that, or had his travel nurse job taught him to fit in?

And why had Anise never achieved that level of comfort, even alone in her own home? "I'll answer your question after you answer mine."

His smile looked sneaky, charmingly conniving. "Deal."

"Okay. Imagine there is an extraordinarily experienced and talented man who lived in the city. He moved to a small town where he didn't know anyone and took a job in a setting he had no experience in. Yet no one—almost no one— would ever guess he was out of his element, because he seems to fit in everywhere he goes. Why is that?"

At the widening of his eyes, she knew he hadn't seen that coming, and she suddenly regretted bringing it up. "I shouldn't have asked. Sometimes I'm too curious for my own good. You don't have to answer."

"No, we made a deal." A twinkle appeared in his eye. "That's a complicated question with a complex answer. Is that man also handsome and buff as a gorilla, and is he sweet and charming and funny?"

His silly grin made her smile. "For argument's sake, let's say he is."

"In that case, that man is not me. So I don't know why he did it. Now you have to answer my question."

How did he always draw laughter from her like water from a well?

"Okay," he said, sobering. "I had to learn to adapt when Martin got hurt. My world changed so fast and so drastically, I had a hard time keeping up at first. I tried to pretend nothing had changed, but that obviously didn't last long. Then I told myself Martin would be better in a couple of days, and everything would go back to normal."

"But you knew that wasn't true."

"Correct. When I admitted the truth, I started helping my parents take care of him. No more sports, no more campouts or hiking or going to the beach. I learned to adapt."

Wow. Anise had always thought she'd adapted well after the tragedies in her life, but maybe she had merely adjusted.

"Now it's your turn. What would you do with your flower farm if you wouldn't have to give up your clinic to do it?"

As honest as he'd been, she had to tell him the truth as well. Anise searched her heart. What would she do with Vestal's Flower Farm?

Suddenly, she knew. "After the plants were healthy again, I'd open a business where people could come and pick their own flowers, and I'd hire someone to work there. Not just anyone—someone who loved flowers and this place as much as I do. I'd fix up Mamaw's house, the way she always wanted it, and maybe even make it a bed-and-breakfast. And when I felt like I didn't belong where I was, I'd go to her house and sit on her porch and smell the same flowers she smelled. It would be a little haven away from the world."

"Tell me why it's your favorite place. I suspect it's not because of the bait store."

Hardly. "Actually, the bait store is the reason I left."

"I'm guessing the fishing worms didn't drive you away."

Anise thought of the rusted metal roof and the chipped-paint wooden siding on the shack that had probably stood there on its crumbling stone foundation for seventy-five years. "I don't know why I haven't had it torn down. Daddy made me quit school and work there when I turned sixteen. My grandmother was long gone by then, and my siblings are all much older and had moved away, so I had no one to talk him out of it."

To her surprise, Harrison's eyes held compassion, not the pity she had seen from others in the past, back when she was young and still talked about it. She'd surprised herself by telling him now.

She hesitated. Might as well tell the whole story. "That bait shop is the reason I needed to leave Mockingbird Creek and the reason I married Vernon. As I said, I was very young, and older guys, in their twenties and thirties, came in every night. Let's just say I was afraid of them. Vernon took advantage of my fear and took me away to Nashville. So I'd tear that place down and put up an arbor and an altar and let people get married there amidst the flowers."

"You'd redeem it."

"Yes, I would."

Harrison's eyes glistened a little. "Tell me about the flowers. Some of them must still be there."

"Sometimes I pick them. Some for our former neighbors, especially Miss Willa Mae, and some for my vases at home."

She thought of the rows of azaleas, camellias, jasmine and just about every other perennial that would grow in Natchez, or so it had seemed when Anise was a girl. All of them now grew wild and untended, needing a good pruning and some fertilizer. Snapdragons, pansies and marigolds continued to reseed themselves, making a colorful tangle of foliage and blossoms.

"Your grandmother was the one who made this your happiest place, wasn't she? Your love for the flower farm might have more to do with the love and safety you felt with her than it does for the flowers or the farm itself."

Either he was highly perceptive, or he'd taken some counseling classes. "Correct. Mama left with another man when I was nine. Daddy sold their trailer, and we moved into Mamaw's house so I could take care of her. She'd already had emphysema for years. I basically became an adult the summer my mother left."

She stopped herself. "Maybe I shouldn't burden you with my past. I never share this information with anybody. Very little of my childhood was happy, and I don't like to tell people about it because it drags them down. I should put it all in the past, but for some reason, I'm not ready to turn loose of the negative things that happened there. And most people probably wouldn't think I had it all that bad. I know that doesn't make any sense."

"Grief and pain often don't make sense." He spoke as if he knew from experience. "Surely you have some good memories of Vestal's Flower Farm."

"My good memories there all involved Mamaw Vestal. I developed a love of flowers because I felt her love when we worked together."

He turned from watching the river, his impossibly blue eyes now searching hers. "I had that kind of love once too, from my dad. That ended when he divorced my mom and moved back East. Now that I think of it, I guess I've spent the rest of my life longing for that kind of love."

Longing for love… "Maybe I have too."

It was as if her view of her whole life suddenly changed. Mamaw's love. Mama and Daddy and Vernon's lack of it. Somehow she'd learned to receive love from her sons and their wives and children and to give love back to them. But love from someone she'd not given birth to or adopted, or her sons hadn't married or fathered? Love on equal footing?

And she thought of Harrison and his failed attempts with Jase. His late wife who couldn't push past her own pain to love Harrison. His father, who'd walked out.

He'd been cheated out of love, just as she had. Yet he'd stayed kind and gentle, despite his pain.

The wind picked up and blew a lock of hair into her face. Anise raised her hand to brush it away, but Harrison beat her to it, his gentle touch reaching her heart as he tucked the hair behind her ear, then slid his hand down to cup her cheek.

"Harrison…"

His eyes softened, and she caught a little shimmer there.

His tender gesture had done something to her heart, something so foreign, so unexpected—so sweet, she didn't want to think about it, didn't want to reason it away. No, she wanted only to savor the moment when she felt cared for, special, comforted.

The rare moment when her heart didn't feel alone.

Quickly, before she could give herself time to think, Anise closed her eyes, reached up and leaned in to Harrison.

And as the river wind picked up and cooled her hot cheeks, she kissed him, long and slow, as if she could kiss away all the pain of their past and all the uncertainty of their future.

He smelled of leather and spice and straw, and as one hand slipped to twine around the back of her neck and the other around her waist, his tenderness made her wrap her arms around him and breathe in the comfort of his embrace. And when he kissed her back, he tasted of sweetened coffee and long-denied dreams that circled around and embedded themselves in this one amazing kiss until—

Oh.

Anise pulled back, cheeks flaming, and covered her face with her hands.

What was she thinking? She'd never even initiated a kiss with Vernon until after they were married.

Why had she done something so impulsive, so irresponsible?

Lowering her hands, she gazed into Harrison's face, confusion clouding his beautiful eyes.

"Anise, it's all right—"

"No." She drew a deep breath, puffed it out, took a few steps back, her eyes stinging. "It's not all right. I don't know why—I'm so sorry."

"Please don't feel sorry." He stepped toward her, reached for her hand.

Anise backed farther from him, unable for a moment to pull her gaze from his eyes, to end the healing in that kiss. Then she turned and ran across the expanse of bridge and onto the ramp, her heels clattering on the wood.

And strengthened her resolve to keep a wide emotional distance from Harrison.

Because being alone was still better than risking another heartbreak.

It was a good thing Harrison had learned navigational skills while he was a traveling nurse, so he could find his way back to the gym for his bike and then home. However, nothing had prepared him for finding his way back to a "friends only" relationship with a woman after he'd kissed her.

Rather, after she'd kissed him.

And what a kiss.

Sure, he could have used the GPS app on his phone, but he didn't feel like having a pushy voice tell him what to do right now. He'd rather hear Anise's gentle voice, the one that always soothed him and made him feel calmer.

He could think when she was around.

Too bad nobody had invented a GPS app that would navigate complicated relationships.

Harrison wanted to follow her to make sure she'd be okay. However, considering the way she'd just literally run from his arms, he doubted she'd welcome his company. She probably wouldn't appreciate him shadowing her either. Since he'd heard her talk to Miss Eugenia about her sunset walks and jogs by the river, she surely felt safe. As she'd said, this was Natchez, not San Diego.

However, it just wasn't in him to leave her defenseless after what happened. That wasn't how real men operated. Although it wouldn't surprise him if Abe had given her self-defense training. Who knew? Maybe she could even take Harrison down.

He ambled down the bridge to the ramp then turned south on Broadway, the direction he'd seen her take. No doubt she was heading home, her Jeep forgotten at the gym. If he couldn't follow close, he'd at least try to keep her in his sight from a distance. Jase had said he was a city slicker, and he was probably right. Harrison didn't know much about small-town life. But he still didn't like her walking alone in the dusk.

As he crossed Canal Street, his phone buzzed. He reached for it, swiped the screen.

A text from Trevor.

Checking in to see how it's going with your son.

He checked the time. Trevor must be home from work. He hit dial.

"Hey. I hear traffic—at least, I think that's what it is. Sounded like just one car. You out-side?" Trevor said as he turned on the video call, getting straight to the point as usual, without a lot of social niceties.

Yeah, Anise did that too. He might get a quick "Hi," but then she usually got right down to business. Strange as it sounded, it put him at ease. He never had to listen to meaningless chatter or complaining or verbal manipulation with her. Or with Trevor.

"I'm outside, all right, walking home alone from a—a situation."

"Sounds like trouble with a woman."

"I don't know what to call it. Not really trouble…it was just a situation."

Trevor walked the phone over to the stove and set it on a stand, and Harrison heard the sound of meat searing in a pan.

Trevor stirred it and added some kind of seasoning. Probably Thai food, his favorite. "We're talking about Anise, right?"

Harrison puffed out a breath. "We were standing on this little footbridge, watching the sun set over the Mississippi River—which, by the way, is unbelievable—and just talking when all of a sudden, she kissed me."

Dead silence.

"Trevor?"

His friend laughed, but Harrison didn't find it funny.

"You say that as if it's a problem," Trevor said through his cackling.

"It *is* a problem. You know I'm not looking for a relationship, and she isn't either. She adopted my son. She's my neighbor. And she's my boss. We even share a dog, sort of. I thought this was complicated before, but now…"

In the distance, Anise had made a right-hand turn. Harrison realized he'd slowed as he talked to Trevor, and he picked up his pace to keep up. She sure could hoof it in those high heels.

"How would you feel about her if she wasn't your son's mother, your boss, and all the rest?"

"It doesn't matter, because she is."

Trevor let out a grunt. "Work with me here."

Harrison grunted back. "Fine. Even if she were some random person I met, say, at church, I wouldn't want a relationship. You know how it went with Lisa. I'd just ruin her life."

"No, you wouldn't, but we'll talk about that another time. Dig deeper." He put water on to boil, a bag of rice noodles sitting on the counter next to the stove. Looked like Trevor was making pad thai again. "What if the problems with Lisa hadn't happened? What if you'd had a happy marriage, then you lost Lisa, and now it's five years later and you meet Anise. What would you do?"

He'd probably hang up the phone, that's what. "I see where you're going, but it doesn't work that way. Besides, Anise sidetracked me so much with that kiss, I haven't told you the big news. Jase figured out who I am."

"You're right, that's big news. How'd it go?"

"Well, he didn't punch me or anything, so it could be worse. Trevor, he wants nothing to do with me, but he did promise Anise that he'd try. So there's that."

His friend made a comforting noise that sounded as if it came from deep within. "I wish it had gone better for you. But it sounds like there's hope. We'll keep praying."

Right.

"Back to that kiss…"

Harrison groaned.

"How do you feel about it?"

"I honestly haven't had time to process it. I mean, she's beautiful and sweet and totally not the kind of woman who goes around kissing guys." Harrison lowered his voice, remembering that he was in a small town and, even though it was getting dark, people might be outside, listening. He dropped his voice to a near whisper. "I can't talk too loud. I don't want her to know I'm following her home."

Maybe he should have thought that through before speaking. It sounded a little creepy. But Trevor would get it.

"Wait—don't you live next door to her?"

Trevor said. "Why are you both walking home, and why aren't you walking with her?"

A grunt rumbled out of Harrison's mouth before he had a chance to stop it. "Everything went sideways after she kissed me. She broke off the kiss and ran off."

"Ran...off?"

"It gets worse. She had this look of horror on her face and said she didn't know why she did it. And then she—" This part hurt. "Then she apologized."

Trevor let out a long, low whistle. "She's falling for you, dude. But she doesn't want it any more than you do."

"No! It's nothing like that. It was just an impulse. We were in a romantic setting, talking about our pasts and how we've always…"

He stopped cold as he remembered his words. *I've spent the rest of my life longing for that kind of love.*

No, no, no…

He watched Anise in the distance, about a block away and still looking as if she could break into a jog at any moment. And she might have, if she hadn't worn those highly impractical yet very cute shoes.

"I have to put a stop to this right away," he said. "I'll tell you the truth, Trevor—I do have feelings for Anise. Not just because she's beautiful."

"You seriously need to ask her out. Tonight."
Trevor still didn't get it.

"I've been around long enough to figure a few things out, and I know that kiss proved she has feelings for me. So I need to protect not just myself, but her too." Harrison watched Anise turn the corner—onto Commerce Street, if he remembered right. "If things were different and I thought I could be a decent husband, I'd ask her out. Tonight. But I won't start something I can't finish. I learned that the hard way with Starr. And Lisa."

"Have it your way. I still predict you'll call me by Thanksgiving and ask me to be your best man." He cheesy-grinned right into the phone, lightening the moment at just the right time, as usual. "Don't wait too long. We're getting old."

Harrison pushed up his sleeve, flexed his bicep. "Does that look old to you?"

"No, sir." Trevor flashed him another smile. "I gotta pay attention to what I'm doing here, or I'll burn dinner. Go catch up with your lady."

His lady. Harrison chose to let that slide.

But as he hung up, not yet close enough to see Anise on the cross street, he wished again for that emotional GPS. Because he and Anise had a long, uncharted journey ahead of them if they hoped to get back to the place they left when she gave him the kiss of his life.

Chapter Seven

Harrison needed to take a deep breath. Slow down. Count to ten. Anything that would calm his nerves and help him stop worrying about what would happen with Jase today and instead keep his focus on the French toast on his griddle. Because any minute, his son would be here to eat breakfast and take the paternity test with him.

Most important, this could be the day Jase would begin to trust him.

He'd warmed the maple syrup, set the table, and prepared blueberries and strawberries for toppings. Two bowls waited on the counter, full of cherry tomatoes, avocados, fresh basil and olive oil. He'd broken four eggs into little individual bowls and heated water to poach them in.

A knock sounded on the front door, setting Harrison's heart pounding.

He turned off the griddle and headed to the living room, Tiny Romeo following.

The little dog must have sensed apprehension in the air, because he'd stayed in the kitchen, lying on the floor close to Harrison, since the alarm went off at five.

The moment he saw Jase, he knew something had changed. The open resentment gone from his face and attitude, he wore a half-hearted smile instead.

Harrison would have preferred a big man-hug, but since that was unrealistic, he'd take the smile.

"I made homemade cinnamon rolls yesterday," Jase said, stepping inside and holding out a round pan covered with plastic wrap.

Harrison took the gift and lifted the plastic. "They smell great. The frosting looks good too."

"I used cream cheese icing this time."

Pulling off the rest of the plastic, Harrison led the way to the kitchen. There he placed the rolls on the table and turned to the stove.

"Are you going to poach those eggs?" Jase asked, eyeing the eggs in their separate bowls and the pot of simmering water.

"I'll drop them as soon as I turn the French toast."

"Want me to cook the eggs?"

Was he serious? Not everybody knew how

to poach. But when Jase picked up the spoon and stirred the water, Harrison figured his son knew what he was doing. "Sure."

Harrison moved to the griddle and turned the toast. Perfect. By the time he put them on a platter, unplugged the griddle and poured coffee, the eggs were done. He brought the avocado bowls to Jase, who lifted out the eggs and slid them into the bowls. Harrison topped them with toasted sesame seeds, black pepper and sea salt flakes, and then they both sat at the table.

After Harrison gave thanks, Jase reached for the dish of softened butter for his French toast.

"I had a talk with Abe last night," Jase said, pouring on syrup. "He reminded me of a...family situation we had a couple years ago."

"A situation?"

"It was a family secret for a little while, but everybody knows now. Seven years ago, Abe and Rosemary eloped."

That didn't sound like a terrible secret.

"They didn't tell anybody about their marriage. Soon they had a fight. Abe took off with the army, and Rosemary moved to St. Simons Island. Problem was, neither of them knew Rosemary was pregnant before she left. Abe was a father for four years and didn't know it."

Harrison sugared his coffee and sipped, unsure what to say about the news.

"Abe told me how hard it was to realize he'd missed the first four years of Georgia's life. He said this is hard for you too, learning you'd had a son for twenty-five years but never knew it until now. And that, if he'd known Georgia existed, he would have done what you did. He would have immediately headed to that island." Jase took a bite from his egg-avocado bowl and washed it down with coffee. "When Abe came over, I'd just spent a long time praying about this, because I wanted to do the right thing."

Harrison set down his forkful of French toast, a hint of hope rising in him. "What's the right thing?"

"To do what I said I'd do. I'm sure you could tell I was halfhearted in my promise to Mama last night. But Abe showed me that wasn't honest. So I'm now willing to give you—give us—an honest chance at a relationship."

Tiny Romeo let out a yowl from the floor at Harrison's feet, the sound he used when he wanted to go next door. Harrison got up and let him out.

"Jase, that's the best news you could give me," he said when he got back to the table. "I've been thinking too, and I want to set your mind at ease about your mom and me. Truth is, she's the most amazing woman I've ever met. And we had a—a moment last night and a kiss. But we both knew immediately that it was wrong, because neither of us is interested in a relationship. We have histories that make us leery of getting close to someone."

Jase's brows rose at the news, and he hesitated. "Mama thinks a lot of you too. But you're right that she's never wanted a relationship after my adoptive father left."

Yes. Harrison leaned in, focused on his son. He'd taken the news of the kiss so well, Harrison wanted nothing more at the moment than to reassure him that it would go no further. "I promise you, if things ever change and I want a romantic relationship with your mom, I will come and tell you myself. Even before I tell her. And if you want me to back off, I will."

Jase nodded, a bit more of the frost leaving his eyes. "I appreciate it."

When the French toast and avocado bowls were gone and they'd polished off as many rolls as they could hold, Harrison retrieved the paternity test kits from the den.

Later, after they'd collected their samples and Jase left for work, Harrison packaged the specimens for shipping. Then he stepped outside and walked with his dog to the shipping company six blocks away.

He opened the box to send the package to the New Orleans lab. With expedited shipping and a fast lab turnaround, they'd have results tomorrow, and then nothing would ever be the same again. And while a part of him trembled at the thought of being a father and grandfather, he knew that getting these results was the right thing to do.

Lord, I'm leaving this in Your hands.

Harrison dropped his package in the box, closed it and didn't look back.

Anise would give her grandmother's vintage Gibson mandolin if it meant she wouldn't have to face Harrison today.

Yesterday, the one bright spot in having the clinic cancelled was that she didn't have to see Harrison. She hid out in her office all day, completing paperwork, updating her board and donors about the clinic's progress and feeling like a fool.

But today, at her desk in the clinic office, she had only about a half hour before his shift began. Her stomach rumbled, but even Harrison's ratatouille couldn't tempt her now. What had she been thinking, kissing him on the bridge? She couldn't know exactly what he thought of her now, but she had a pretty good idea. And she didn't like it.

Worse, she had a feeling she'd never get that kiss out of her mind. Who knew a kiss could be like that, taking her breath, healing her heart—making her whole?

And invading her mind. Because as hard as she tried, she couldn't stop thinking about it.

Also driving her anxiety was the fact that the paternity test results could come today, since Jase had said Harrison chose a twenty-four-hour lab. She lifted her glass of raspberry sparkling water, but the ice had melted and it was room temperature. She set it down and shoved it away.

Anise glanced at her watch. Harrison was always early, so it was time to check her hair after wearing her helmet during the scooter ride to work. Not that she wanted another look at her sleep-deprived, pale face and puffy eyes. On the other hand, she also didn't want today's patients to see her looking a mess and half sick. If they did, they might wonder if the nurse practitioner needed a doctor.

She retrieved her mirror from the middle drawer of her desk and secured a few loose bobby pins in her messy bun, then she glanced at the clock over her desk.

The sound of the doorknob turning made her heart lurch.

She slid the mirror into the drawer, then swiveled her chair to face him, catching sight of his tender smile. He probably intended that smile to make her feel less foolish and to take the edge off her fear of this conversation. But it fell short. Far short.

Harrison carried two white paper sacks into the office. He handed one to her and placed the other on his desk. "You look like you got a lot more sleep than I did."

What? She looked a mess. But it was kind of him to say. She picked up the sack and found it heavier than it looked. "What's in here?"

"I thought that, if I'm going to live in Natchez, I need to start eating Southern food. I never had much of that in California, especially grits. I wanted to give them a try, so I picked up breakfast."

Anise lifted the to-go containers from the sack and found biscuits, gravy, bacon and grits. The best comfort food—and the best "dispel the awkwardness" food—in the world.

And that was good, because it would be hard for even the greatest Southern food to break through the discomfiture wafting through the room along with the aroma of bacon.

She emptied her sack of a packet of plastic cutlery, napkins and condiments. When she opened her foam bowl of gravy, savory steam rolled out. "You must have known I came in early."

"I heard your scooter." Harrison set his food

on his desk, then he took off his jacket and hung it on the back of his chair.

As nice as it was to have breakfast delivered, Anise knew it would stick in her throat if she tried to eat with this awkwardness between them. If only they could go back to the way things were before the kiss. But that wouldn't happen.

Because once you kissed someone, everything changed forever.

Anise shielded her eyes with her hand for an instant as she breathed a quick prayer. Here in this room, she was Harrison's boss. Their current situation would impact their work if they didn't resolve it. So it was up to her to open the conversation.

Which she would gladly do, if she had any idea how.

Jesus, give me words.

She looked up at him as he sat down and pulled out his breakfast. "Harrison, I'm embarrassed and humiliated to have to bring up the subject of the other night. I wasn't thinking, and I don't—"

Wait, what was he doing with that bowl of gravy? She stared for a moment in horror, then found her voice. "Stop!"

He froze, eyes wide. "What? What's wrong?"

Anise pointed at the foam bowl in his hand, lid off, gravy flowing onto—

His grits.

"Set the gravy down, Harrison."

His mouth opened, slightly at first and then wider. "Anise, what are you talking about?"

This morning was shaping up worse than she thought. She got up and bounded over to his desk. "In the South, we do not put gravy on grits. Ever. Gravy goes on biscuits. Salt, pepper and butter go on grits."

He gave her a sidewise look, eyebrows lifted almost to his scalp. "Is that…a law?"

She sighed. "Harrison, if you're going to live in Natchez, you have to know certain things about Southern food. This is about as basic as it gets."

"Ohh-kay."

Anise took his spoon and scraped as much gravy off the grits as she could, taking a lot of the grits with it. Then she used his knife to put butter on the untainted delicacy that remained and put the rest of the gravy on one of his split biscuits.

"This is dreadful. Half of your gravy is ruined." She strode to her desk and picked up her own bowl of creamy gravy. She dipped her spoon into it and covered his other biscuit. "There."

One corner of his mouth turned upward in a

half grin. "I take it that grits etiquette is of utmost importance in this town."

"In the whole South. This is even worse than putting milk and sugar on them like some people do up north. I'm just glad Jase didn't see that. We have enough trouble with him as it is."

Oh, my word. Did Miss Eugenia's voice just come out of Anise's mouth?

The huge grin on his face told her he'd heard the similarity too.

It was beyond time to change the subject.

If only he'd brought doughnuts—anything— instead. But for now, she had to clear the air and determine whether or not she'd destroyed their working relationship two nights ago.

"We have something more important to talk about." She dropped her gaze, unable to meet his eyes. "The day I hired you, Tara, the director of nursing, wanted to know if you and I would feel awkward, working together. And yes, what I did the other night makes me feel over-the-top awkward. I need to know whether you still feel comfortable working with me."

"Anise." His deep, melodious voice drew her attention back to him. "Don't worry. As far as I'm concerned, we're good. I enjoy working with you, I believe in the clinic and I want to continue."

"But I was so out of line, and I don't even

know why I did it. I've never done anything like that before. It was all my fault."

He gave her a slow smile. "No, it wasn't. I guess you didn't notice, but I kissed you back."

He certainly had. Her face flamed a little at the thought and at his expression. "I wasn't trying to start something. It's just that we shared the same experience, longing for and looking for love all our lives, and I just…"

"It's okay. What if we put that kiss behind us and move on from here?" He stood and faced her, close enough she could see the gray flecks in his blue eyes. "Anise, you're smart and kind and beautiful, but twelve years of marriage taught me that I'm not husband material. I didn't have what it took to make my late wife happy, and that's one mistake I refuse to repeat. It's one thing to mess up my own life, but I'm not willing to risk making a third woman miserable."

He had to be wrong about that. Sure, he'd been young and irresponsible with Starr, but she couldn't help thinking a lot of Lisa's unhappiness might have been her own fault. Certainly her infertility wasn't her fault. But perhaps her attitude was.

At any rate, it wasn't her place to say.

Harrison sat at his desk again and typed on his keyboard for a few seconds. Moments later, he stopped. "I have an email about the paternity test. The results are here."

She put her hand to her chest. "I think my heart stopped for a moment."

"Mine too," he said in a near whisper. After a couple of mouse clicks, he gestured for her to come over. "Let's look at it together."

Anise quick-stepped to his desk and stood behind him, riveting her gaze on the screen as he opened the document.

Probability of paternity: 99.999998%.

She watched the change in his eyes as his expression morphed from uncertainty to something bigger, something fine and noble. It was as if he'd suddenly found his purpose, his reason for living.

"It's settled, Anise." His deep voice held a little tremor. "Just as we thought, I'm Jase's father."

Settled. Yes.

That's when it hit her. At some point, she'd realized Harrison would be a great father for Jase. She'd have been thrilled for her son if that kiss hadn't happened. But she'd spoiled everything. After her foolishness on the bridge, it would have been easier for her if it had all been a mistake.

But it wasn't a mistake. Anise was staring right at the evidence. She had to face reality—

and that reality wasn't okay with her. It meant Harrison would probably stay in Natchez for the rest of his life, attending family functions, singing in the choir, living next door to her. Right now, with her awkwardness with Harrison so new and poignant, she couldn't imagine living with it for the rest of her life.

Would her embarrassment and regret fade with time? Yes, she'd learned that from experience. But she didn't know when or how much.

However, she did know that her next words could color Harrison's relationship with Jase for years to come. *Jesus, give me words...*

That's when clarity hit her—it had to be okay with her.

She had to accept the truth and embrace it, to make a decision that yes, this was okay, that the good outweighed the bad. As she well knew, the feelings would eventually follow.

She couldn't let her emotions stand in the way of Harrison becoming a great father to Jase. And of Jase being a great son to Harrison.

Anise drew a deep breath, purposefully changing her attitude and her mind. She laid her hand on his shoulder and spoke new truth. "Harrison, I'm truly happy."

His eyes misted a bit, melting her heart. "I promise to be the best father to him that I—"

A knock sounded on the office door and interrupted him. "Mama?"

Jase.

Anise snatched her hand from Harrison's shoulder, hoping their faces wouldn't betray the fact that they'd shared a tender moment. Again. She called for him to come in.

The door swung open, and he stuck in his head. "Hey, Harrison. Mama, I just have a minute, but I wanted to let you know—" His gaze shot from her to Harrison and back. "What's wrong? Did something happen?"

Perceptive as always. Anise turned to Harrison and nodded, silently inviting him to give Jase the news.

Harrison cleared his throat. "Jase, have you checked your email today?"

"Not yet. I stopped in to check on Joseph before the deacons' meeting this morning."

"We have the test results," Harrison said. "Would you like to see the report? Or would you rather read it in private?"

Jase visibly swallowed, then he came the rest of the way in the office and shut the door. "I'll read it here. I already know what it'll say."

Since the result was at the top of the page, written in red, it took only a moment for his life to change forever. Just as Anise's and Harrison's had minutes before.

"It's official." Jase smiled at her, that little smile he used to put on when he was a boy and things were particularly hard at home. He'd always meant to make her feel better with that smile. Now he shifted his gaze to Harrison. "Guess you're stuck with me."

Harrison just clasped Jase's shoulder in what looked like silent encouragement.

Considering Jase's previous animosity toward Harrison, Anise chose to be grateful for his lackluster response. "If you want, you can tell everybody tonight at family night. Unless you'd rather wait."

"I guess we should tell them." He turned to Harrison. "But I still need to get to know you better. I'm not ready to jump into a father-son relationship."

From his tone, he might as well have also said he wasn't ready for Harrison to have a grandfather-granddaughter relationship with Bella.

"Fair enough," Harrison said.

"We can't have family night tonight, though," Jase said on his way to the door. "Joseph is scheduled for discharge from the hospital late this afternoon, and I'm taking him home and getting him settled. We also have a wedding at Wisteria Chapel this weekend, and I'm meeting with the bride and groom after lunch and the photographer later this afternoon, so I won't have time to cook. It's too late to ask anyone else to step in or to get catering for thirty people."

Harrison glanced at Anise. "Thirty? Do you have more family that I don't know about?"

"It's not just the family anymore," Jase said. "It started as me, Mama and Abe. But now we invite the church youth group and Pastor David and some church people who don't have relatives nearby. We don't like anybody to be lonely."

Harrison pulled a sheet of paper from his file drawer and a pen from his pocket and started scribbling what looked like a grocery list. "I can go straight to the store after work and make a taco bar for the whole crowd. That's quick and easy."

That made her pastor-son's smile light up. "That would be great. I invited a new family in church to come tonight. They just moved here from Vicksburg, and I dreaded telling them we weren't having it."

"I can help. I'll cut up the vegetables while you cook the meat," Anise said.

"You can't carry a whole taco bar on your Harley," Jase said. "Mama, can you drive him?"

Harrison shook his head. "I have a dog now, and I'm tired of bumming rides when I take him along. So I bought a Bronco yesterday."

Jase held out his hand. "Harrison, this means a lot to me. Thank you."

Oh, her son knew exactly how to wreck her. She blinked away the stinging in her eyes, feeling an inch closer to a place of hope.

Five minutes into family night, Harrison was convinced that his son truly was called to the ministry.

So far, he'd counted twelve Armstrong family members—both immediate and extended—seven teenagers, Pastor David, choir director Zeke, eight friends, and five dogs at the big old mansion where his son lived, worked and performed destination weddings.

The size of the crowd and the estate didn't impress him. His son's love for these people did, especially the way Jase interacted with the teens. Harrison didn't have to watch or listen long to see that he was a father figure to these kids, and he might be the only father some of them had.

Maybe his son would be the one to teach Harrison how to be a father.

And a grandfather.

Jase had texted earlier to offer him the use of Rosewood's huge kitchen, so now Harrison added his homemade taco seasoning to the giant iron skillets of ground beef and chicken he'd cooked to perfection. Hunger pangs hit him as the spices mixed and filled the room with an amazing aroma.

Anise stood at a wooden cutting board at the counter, dicing tomatoes for her homemade fresh salsa. She turned to him with a smile, and he hoped she hadn't heard his rumblings.

"I can't take my mind off your news and Jase's change of heart," she said. "He's coming around."

"I need to focus on cooking, but Jase is all I can think about. Let's hope I didn't use a cup of chili powder instead of a tablespoon in the meat."

"Tonight is going to be a huge victory for you both. You're speaking his love language—cooking and eating."

Love language, huh? Maybe cooking was Harrison's language too, because he loved working in the kitchen with Anise. She seemed to give special attention to each task she did, taking time to make every dish as delicious as she could. From all he'd seen in her, he guessed she showed her love by serving people.

She undoubtedly had no idea how attractive that made her. If things were different...

But things were not different. And he had to admit it was getting harder and harder for him to remember that. Especially since the kiss.

Yeah, the kiss...

Nursing school had trained him to drive away all thoughts and emotions that could distract him from his mission. He must have let that skill grow rusty, though, because keeping that mind-shattering kiss from the forefront of his thoughts had become nearly impossible at times.

Like now, when she finished stirring her salsa, scooped up a big spoonful and took a bite. Her eyes closed, she let out a soft sound somewhere between a hum and a sigh.

Harrison hid his grin and averted his gaze, in case she opened her eyes and saw him watching her. This woman sure loved her food.

"Want to try it?" At his nod, she took a clean spoon from the drawer and loaded it up.

He took it and tested the salsa. The tomatoes tasted fresh and ripe, and she'd added just the right amount of sea salt, cilantro and lime juice. "This is amazing," he said. "I need more."

Her laughter touched his heart as she opened a bag of chips and offered it to him. Soft and sweet, her laugh always seemed to soothe him, make him feel secure—warm.

With their jobs and the Jase connection forcing them to spend so much time together, he'd have to learn to curb his attraction to Anise, to stifle his emotions. Because although they'd known each other only a week, this woman could easily win his heart.

If he let her. Which he couldn't.

He and Anise set out the taco bar in the formal dining room—who knew some old mansions had two dining rooms?—and then wandered into the oversized room Jase called the center hall. With its comfortable-looking couches and chairs, piano and big tables holding different games and puzzles, it didn't look like a hall to Harrison. But all the other rooms in this part of the house opened into this one, so in a sense, he could see it.

They sat on the couch next to an elderly lady who played peekaboo with Bella, and Anise introduced her as Miss Fannie Swan, the lady of the house.

"Oh, you're Harrison!" she said in a lilting Southern accent. "I've been waiting for you. Eugenia told me all about you."

Bella grabbed both of Miss Fannie's hands and lifted them to the older lady's face, clearly wanting to continue the game. Miss Fannie covered and uncovered her eyes and made Bella laugh as a couple of teen girls raced by, giggling.

Harrison laughed too. "I think she believes you're her grandmother."

"At my age, I could be her great-great-grandmother." She glanced around, then lowered her voice. "Would you like to hold her?"

Hold her? When was the last time he'd held a child? Maybe ten years ago, when some of his and Lisa's friends had started having children, and they'd dropped one on his lap and laughed at his awkwardness.

But this was Bella. His granddaughter. "Do you think Jase would mind?"

Miss Fannie's laugh tinkled like a crystal bell. "Of course not. You're her—"

She stopped herself, glancing around the room. "You're…sitting right here, just when I need to rest from our games."

Harrison held back a grin as Miss Fannie tried to extricate herself from her gaffe. Clearly, she knew exactly who Harrison was, but she hadn't figured it out on her own. He glanced at Miss Eugenia, who played a board game with Georgia at the next table. She met his gaze and gave him a look he assumed she meant as innocent.

She didn't fool Harrison. Miss Eugenia had a part in this little slip of the tongue. She must have figured out their secret at choir practice.

"I don't know much about babies," he said, shifting his gaze to Miss Fannie.

"That's all right. Erin and I taught Jase how to take care of her, starting when she was three days old. I'll help you too, if you need it." She handed the child to him.

He took Bella in his arms, feeling a bit clumsy. But when she leaned against his chest and stuck her thumb in her mouth, his discomfort vanished in the wake of the emotional tsunami crashing through his heart.

He was holding his granddaughter. His family. His legacy.

Heavy footsteps pounded down the spiral stairs in the corner, and the next thing Harrison knew, Jase was in the room, stopping next to Harrison and seeming bigger than life in his home and his ministry setting.

Lord, I don't know why You gave me this amazing son and this beautiful granddaughter, but I thank You for them.

"Want to stand up with me while I introduce you, Harrison?" Jase said.

Even though he knew Jase's motivation for introducing him was because of his sense that it was the right thing to do and nothing personal, Harrison was happy to be asked to stand with his son. He struggled for a moment, trying to get up and not drop Bella.

"Let me help you," Jase said, reaching over and taking the child from Harrison's arms. "Sitting with her is the easy part. I remember what it was like to learn to stand up while holding her."

"Thanks. I admit I don't know what I'm doing when it comes to children."

When Harrison was on his feet, Jase handed Bella back to him. "You'll get the hang of it."

Despite his apprehension, Harrison chose to believe he would.

"Y'all listen up," Jase called to the family and guests, some sitting around and playing games in the center hall and some in the dining room, eyeing the food. "If you haven't met him already, this is Harrison Mitchell. We have a surprise. Harrison plans to stay in Natchez for a while because he is my birth father and Bella's grandfather."

Harrison wasn't sure what kind of response he'd expected, but this uncomfortable dead silence wasn't it.

He felt as if he should say something, break the silence, alleviate the awkwardness. But for the life of him, he couldn't think of a word to say. Apparently, Jase couldn't either, because the uncomfortable quiet stretched on.

Then Anise stood and, in her tactful manner, brought a sense of calm with her sweet smile and her quiet way of grounding him. Of grounding her family and everyone she cared about.

"Some of you remember when Vernon and I came back from Nashville with one-year-old Abe and newborn Jase, whom we'd adopted. My dear friend Starr was his birth mother. She trusted me to be a mother to her child. Raising

Jase and Abe has been the biggest joy of my life." She brushed her hand across Bella's dark hair as the child still snuggled up against Harrison. "Now I'm happy that I get to share Jase, Erin, Bella and the new babies with Jase's natural father."

When Anise sat down, the sense of anticipation in the room escalated as if the whole crowd paused to hear what Harrison would say. He sent a quick, silent prayer, unsure how to follow Anise's gracious speech. "I'm proud of the man my son has become, and I'm grateful to Anise and Vernon and everybody who stepped up to help them do the job that should have fallen to me." That *would* have fallen to him, had he known. He landed his gaze on Miss Eugenia and held it there, hoping she understood he was silently thanking her, since doing so out loud would betray Anise's confidence.

The older lady held his gaze, touched her hand to her heart, and nodded.

Yes, she knew.

Jase gave thanks for the food and invited the guests to help themselves to dinner—or "supper," as he called it—and then he stayed by Harrison's side and introduced him to guests he hadn't met.

After the crowd demolished the taco bar, the six banana-caramel, chocolate meringue and lemon pies and most of a hummingbird cake, the teens cleaned up the mess—cheerfully, for a pack of junior high kids. When they'd finished, Jase gave a short devotion centered around the Bible story of a Pharisee named Nicodemus coming to Jesus at night and asking Him an important question. Then Jase led them all in prayer.

Chaos broke out when they divided into teams of four for a game they called Hounds Head. Having given sleepy Bella to Erin, Harrison ended up on a team with Zeke and teen boys named Darnell Covington and Chance Boyer.

"We're gonna win with you on our team, Mr. Harrison. You'll be great at horseshoes!" Chance all but shouted while admiring Harrison's biceps.

"I appreciate that, but Zeke's the one who'll get the win," Harrison said, indicating Zeke's impressive guns. "I've never played horseshoes before."

They looked at him as if he'd said he'd never eaten grits before. Which he hadn't before today.

"Why not?" Darnell asked.

He wasn't sure. "Maybe city people don't play horseshoes. At any rate, I never knew anybody who played it."

Darnell shook his head, but Chance piped up, "Then I don't ever want to live in a city."

Jase got everybody's attention with a whistle through his teeth. "The object of the game is to rack up as many points as you can before Miss Fannie calls time." He paused to let the elderly lady wave the old-fashioned megaphone in her hand. "Each team has five minutes at each game station to get as many points as we can. Start us, Miss Fannie."

"Take your places," Miss Fannie called through the megaphone. "Thirty seconds!"

"Come on! Let's get to the horseshoes before somebody else does." Chance bolted toward the back door, Darnell running behind him.

Zeke glanced at Harrison and shrugged, then the two men jogged to the door and met the boys outside.

Within moments, they heard Miss Fannie's amplified voice through the screen door. "Ready, go!"

Zeke seemed a little on the laid-back side, but to Harrison's surprise, the choir director was as competitive as he was, and their team scored the win for the first round.

In the second round, they threw indoor magnetic darts. Before the first ten seconds were up, Harrison understood Hounds Head's offbeat name. All five dogs, including Sugar and Tiny Romeo, raised a ruckus in the center hall, running around and barking.

He tried to control his dog, but Miss Fannie just laughed. "That's part of the fun. When we started playing this game, we had only my golden retriever, Sunny, and she ran around and stuck her head into every station—Dutch Blitz, Jenga, Throw Throw Burrito. It didn't matter what they played, she was in the middle of it. Just like tonight, except we now have five dogs. Hence, the name Hounds Head."

Later, after Miss Fannie declared Harrison's team the winners and rewarded them with milkshake gift cards from the Malt Shop, Abe approached Harrison. "Now I see the resemblance between you and Jase."

"If you think we look alike, wait until you hear us sing together. That's what clenched it for Jase."

"I'm never skipping choir practice again. We've never had a situation like that before." Abe grinned at him, then sobered. "I want you to know I'm glad to have you as my…what? Can I think of you as an uncle?"

An uncle…

Harrison realized then that he'd been so caught up in Jase, he hadn't stopped to think about his relationship with Abe. But he already liked Abe—a lot. "I'm proud to have you as family—to be like an uncle to you. I don't have any living siblings, and my late wife was an only child, so I never thought I'd be an uncle."

Now he needed to learn how to be a father, a grandfather and an uncle. This was getting complicated in a good sort of way.

"We have a few uncles and aunts," Abe said. "Most of them live away from here, so we don't see them much or have a relationship with them."

Interesting how quickly Harrison kept gaining new family here in Natchez. And how much he liked it.

Driving home later, Tiny Romeo in the seat beside him, Harrison couldn't get the word *family* off his mind. If he was honest with himself, he'd known for a long time that, by having no extended family, he'd missed out on something important. But the knowledge that he had a son, especially a son who looked so much like him, had intensified his need for a family. What Jase wouldn't know, and what would be difficult for Harrison to explain, was his insecurity about this whole thing and the fear that Jase would think he was still the man he used to be—a man who didn't stick around.

He thought about his last in-person conversation with Trevor, just before Harrison left San Diego. His words to Trevor echoed through his mind with a vengeance.

I have to go. To think that I might have a son—this is too big to ignore. Even if I can't find him, I have to try, or I'll regret it the rest of my life.

Sure, he'd thought the stakes were high when he'd straddled his bike and started the long drive to Natchez. But the moment he saw Jase, everything changed. Then everything changed again when he met Bella—except more.

Without doubt, nothing would ever be the same again.

Who'd have ever thought someone would one day call Harrison grandpa? The way the little girl chattered through dinner, he knew she'd pick it up right away.

Grandpa. Yes, that's what he'd have her call him. Not a name that was supposed to keep a man from feeling old. He'd be a solid, dependable, loving Grandpa, just as he remembered Grandpa Richard had been during the few times Harrison had seen him, on the older man's annual trips from his Maine hometown.

But first Harrison somehow had to build a relationship with his son, and not only so he could become involved in Bella's life. No, he wanted Jase as family as much as he wanted Bella—and the new babies. And Abe for an honorary nephew.

The realization hit him in the gut. At this

moment, he wanted nothing more than to have a family.

A real family.

Was this what Lisa had felt? Did this emotion drive her to try everything from home remedies to daily temperature readings to fertility drugs to in vitro fertilization? Back then, he'd thought a baby would be great, but he'd never experienced Lisa's desperation for a child. He never told her, but he'd been sure he'd be just as happy without a child as with one.

But now, Harrison somehow knew his freedom, his career, and his comfortable single-guy life would never again satisfy him.

Lord, I think I finally understand my wife.

About a decade too late.

Chapter Eight

A few minutes before seven on Homecoming Sunday morning, Anise pulled into the church parking lot for her shift in the kitchen, wondering if she had the time wrong. There should have been eight or nine more cars here by now.

Had the six o'clock shift not shown up?

Anise hurried to grab her tote bags with her contribution of raw vegetables and dip and six loaves of her homemade bread and muscadine jelly, along with her favorite paring knife, just in case. She got out of the Jeep and strode to the canopy and into the foyer. By now, the first-shift workers should have had green beans and corn cooked and waiting in the bins of the warming tables, and she should have smelled potatoes cooking so the second shift could mash and season them. But no inviting aromas greeted her inside the church.

Pastor David met her on his way to his office. "You'd better get to the kitchen and help Jase."

"What happened? There should be twice as many cars in the parking lot."

"There's a case of stomach flu going around. So far, five families have called and said they're too sick to make it today."

"How many of those families include kitchen workers?"

"All of them," Pastor David said over his shoulder as he approached his office. "I came up here for my phone so I can call around to find help."

Anise took the steps to the kitchen at a run and soon found a half dozen food service–sized cans of corn and green beans sitting unopened next to one of the stoves. Empty pork and bean cans lay on the counter next to two huge baking pans full of as-yet-unseasoned beans. Two empty soup kettles and boxes of macaroni took up most of the counter space by the sinks.

Jase sat perched on a stool, potato peels flying as if the whole Homecoming dinner depended on him alone.

And it had, until Anise got there.

It was a good thing she'd brought her best knife. She set her tote bags on a nearby table, snatched an apron from the top drawer by the sink and put it on. "I just talked to Pastor David.

He's going to make some calls and try to get you some help."

"Well, I've already called everybody," Jase said, looking up from the potatoes. "The only way he's going to get any more help is to call Hope Fellowship on the next corner and borrow some members."

Anise smiled at his attempt at humor. She grabbed a potato and a pan to peel into and dug in. "Rosemary has her hands full on Sunday mornings, with three small children, so we can't ask her."

"And we're not asking Abe. He'll put curry in the milk gravy."

True. "Erin's close to her due date, so we shouldn't bother her either."

"Mama, Erin's only kitchen skills are making salad and washing dishes."

Also true.

"There's Miss Eugenia—"

"Already thought of that. It's too dark for her to drive her golf cart, and the judge and Miss Cozette don't like to drive in the dark either. I called Abe, but the whole family was still in bed. They'll be another forty-five minutes."

The obvious solution finally came to her. "Jase, what about Harrison? He can pick up Miss Eugenia, then we'd have two extra sets of hands. He's a great cook."

Jase shook his head. "There's a big difference between making tacos and preparing a full-on Southern Sunday dinner with fried chicken, homemade gravy and biscuits made from scratch."

Anise pulled out her phone and hit Harrison's picture icon. "You have fifty pounds of potatoes sitting here. Harrison and Miss Eugenia can peel and quarter them and put them on to cook. When they're done, they can mash them. You and I can fry the chicken and make gravy, and when they're done with the potatoes, Miss Eugenia can show Harrison how to make the biscuits. Pastor David will help too. He might not know how to cook, but he can follow our instructions. And wash dishes."

"When Harrison and Miss Eugenia get here," Jase said, his voice holding a little less defeat than it had a few moments ago, "you can finish the beans, and I'll get the macaroni and cheese ready for the oven. That way, they can both bake slowly."

Harrison answered, and when Anise explained the situation, he promised to call Miss Eugenia and pick her up.

"Mama, you've solved the biggest problem," Jase said as Anise started peeling potatoes again. "But we've also lost most of our choir, including Joseph. And Abe and I were supposed to sing a trio with JD Turner, but he's sick too. We're short on special music, which is a tragedy on Homecoming Sunday."

Anise wasn't too disappointed about JD not showing up, since he hadn't been exactly cordial back when Abe rented JD's building for the gym. Even though Abe bought the space from him last year, and even though Anise had forgiven him, things were still tense when JD was around.

But Jase was right about Homecoming. Although the shortage of musicians wasn't technically a tragedy, the church did expect dozens of former members who had moved away but came home every year to visit lifelong friends, hear the district superintendent preach and listen to a lot of great music. "At least we still have our speaker."

Pastor David walked in and grabbed a potato peeler from a drawer. He pulled up a stool and started to peel, joining the conversation as if he'd been there all along. "He'll be good, all right," he said. "Pastor Bronson Maguire is a no-nonsense, no-compromise preacher with a giant heart for people."

"But we still need more music." Anise finished peeling a potato, rinsed it in the sink and laid it on the big cutting board. "What about Harrison? Could he sing the harmony on the song you and Abe were going to sing with JD?"

"I thought of that." Jase shook his head. "He could if he had time to learn it. But it's not an easy harmony part. And we can't ask him to sing melody because it's a tenor part. Abe has to do that."

Harrison and Miss Eugenia arrived moments later, and as they took over the potatoes, Jase told them about their musical dilemma.

"I don't know that song, but if you get me the lyrics, we can run through it here while we work, and I'll improvise the harmony," he said as if he wasn't talking about something few musicians could pull off. "That way, I can focus on memorizing the words and creating a harmony line while I peel potatoes."

Did he realize how over-the-top that sounded?

Jase ran upstairs for the sheet music, and before she knew it, her son and his father belted out a beautiful impromptu arrangement of a hymn so old, she'd never heard it, and so deep, it touched a place in her heart she'd protected for decades.

The richness, the emotion in the two men's identical voices brought a sting to Anise's eyes. She caught the admiration on Jase's face, the same expression she'd seen Thursday night when Harrison interacted with Darnell and Chance, two boys with rough backgrounds who tried their best to follow Jesus.

When she'd told Harrison that food was Jase's love language, she'd misspoken. Jase's love language was showing the love of the Lord to his youth group. And Harrison seemed to step right into that role, even praying with the two teens at the end of the night and offering to help them figure out the math homework they struggled with.

When they had the food in the warming tables and the kitchen cleaned, they headed upstairs to the packed sanctuary. Anise and Harrison joined the family in their usual seats while Jase moved from row to row, greeting visitors and members. Zeke opened the song service with a contemporary worship song and then transitioned to a classic hymn. Sharing a hymnal with Harrison, Anise melted a little at the sound of his bass voice so near to her ear.

When the time came for her song with Jase, she squeezed out to the aisle, carrying the ancient hymnal Jase had brought her. She played the intro to "Just Over in the Gloryland," and when they sang the comforting, happy words of the old song, a new joy infused their voices—a joy that somehow dispelled the old memories of singing through sorrow and now felt more like a celebration of brighter days and clearer vision.

How could a century-old song touch her heart this way?

Maybe because the glory land wasn't just in the sweet by and by. Was it possible that the glory land could start in the here and now?

As they moved into the third verse, Anise let the mood and tempo carry her to a place of deeper joy. Something had changed within her heart between the time she'd played this song with Jase at her house and this present moment. She didn't know what it was, but she knew it was powerful, life changing—life giving.

And she liked it.

On impulse, during the last chorus, Anise glanced out at the congregation and caught Harrison's gaze upon her as they transitioned into the bridge. A tender gaze, one filled with emotion, perhaps gratitude.

Then she understood.

The Lord was using this situation with Harrison and Jase to begin to change them all. It was making Jase softer and challenging him to stretch, to open his heart to another father. It was shifting Harrison's priorities, putting work in a less important place than people and giving him confidence to love his new family.

It was even dispelling Anise's fears of more abandonment and prodding her to take another chance at a relationship with a man.

She'd never thought that would happen.

Anise scanned the rest of the congregation

and sensed that they too were experiencing the presence of the Lord.

As they wound up the song, ending with an even bigger and more powerful ending than the one she'd played with Jase at home, the congregation bounded to their feet, applauding and praising the Lord for His great gift of the glory land before she'd even hit the last measure.

And Anise praised with them, her heart full and her future bright.

In his den late that night, Harrison sank into the thickly padded cushions in his leather recliner and tried to focus on his new detective novel, but he couldn't care less whodunit. The church service had been spectacular, he'd had an opportunity to help his son, and he got to listen to and take part in some great music. He couldn't have asked for more from a small-town get-together.

Or a big-city one, for that matter.

At the pattering of rain on the window, he tried to convince himself that the service, not Anise, was the reason he'd had such a great time.

He smiled at the memory of Anise calling him for help when the church kitchen had all but shut down, and how she'd held the other side of the hymnal with him during the service. And when she'd played and sung that old-time hymn with Jase, it had sounded even better than it had in her house on that recent day that seemed a lifetime ago.

Now he tried to remember his routine in San Diego and before. What had he done with his time back then? What meaningful things had happened to him since Lisa passed? He couldn't remember.

Harrison reached for his sweet tea from the side table next to him and gulped half the glass, listening to a low rumble of thunder. Had his entire focus shrunk to nothing more than one flight after another, one nursing shift after another, one critical patient after another, with church twice a week and a few get-togethers a month with friends?

For the first time, he realized how one-dimensional his heart had become after Lisa passed away. How meaningless, even self-centered.

It was time to admit that his feelings had changed toward life—toward Anise—today.

But no, the more he thought about it, he realized those emotions had been there for a while. Probably since the moment he saw her on the porch, her hair down and long and beautiful, a charming look of surprise in her soft brown eyes as he leaped into her backyard, looking as foolish as he'd ever been. Then she'd made him feel relaxed and secure in the face of his embarrassment when that gorilla picture of him came out on social media.

She'd even helped him through the awkwardness of that epic choir practice gone wrong.

It was time to…

He couldn't finish the thought, his throat tightening. Despite the ache growing in his chest, he drew a deep breath. Slowly, he blew it out, sweat beading up on his scalp.

It was time to ask her out.

Harrison bounded from his chair and paced into the hall. Maybe he should go for a long run in the rain. Then work out for a couple hours. Then run again. Surely that would dispel either his idea of asking her out or his fear of it.

He strode to the kitchen, looked out the window facing Anise's house and caught sight of her through her kitchen glass. While he couldn't tell what she was doing, she looked busy, as always. Maybe she was cooking for someone in her family or her circle of friends. Or stirring up a snack to have while she read a novel tonight. Either way, merely seeing her through the window gave him a sense of comfort.

Yeah, he was in trouble.

Maybe, if he did nothing, she'd kiss him again. That way, he wouldn't have to make the next move.

Or not. Because he had a feeling that wasn't going to happen. No, he had to decide whether to ask Anise out and risk ruining everything, or hold his peace and miss out on the chance of a lifetime.

When sprinkles of rain turned to a deluge, he couldn't see her anymore, so he moved from the window and rooted around in his refrigerator instead. While he wasn't one to comfort himself with food, it seemed like a good idea tonight. He found a leftover fried chicken leg, mashed potatoes and gravy from the church dinner and warmed them in the microwave.

Who knew Southern cooking was this good?

When the timer went off, he sat at his small cherry table in the little area off the kitchen, the one Miss Eugenia had called the breakfast nook, and saw Anise in her window again.

If his landlady was the mysterious Natchez matchmaker, she was a pro at it.

As he indulged in the tender chicken and creamy potatoes and gravy, he tried to think of a special place to take Anise.

Boat ride on the river?

That wouldn't be special, since she'd lived near the Mississippi River all her life.

Motorcycle ride somewhere?

No. She puttered around on a scooter every

day, so Anise probably wouldn't be impressed with his Harley.

One by one, Harrison rejected every bad idea that came to him. Why was this so hard? All he wanted to do was to think of the perfect…

Date.

There. He'd finally said the word, at least in his mind.

Harrison checked his watch. It was still early in California. He loaded his dirty plate and fork into the dishwasher and headed back to the den and his favorite chair. There he set his book on the antique sea chest opposite the chair and flopped down. He reached for the phone and called Trevor.

"How was your special service this morning?" Trevor asked. He must have clicked his phone's video button, because his face filled Harrison's screen for a moment before his friend put it on its stand. "What did you call it?"

"Homecoming. I guess it's a country-church thing. But it was good. The church was so packed, the ushers had to put folding chairs in the aisles. Anise played a lively old hymn on the piano, and she and Jase sang."

"How'd it sound?"

Harrison could see his friend sitting alone in his den, just as Harrison was in his. "I can't describe it. Full of heart, exuding joy born of sorrows. It was as if those two had written the song from their experiences."

"Yeah? How'd she look?"

What? "Trevor, you have a one-track mind."

Trevor cackled in his ear. "I can tell she looked good just by hearing you talk about her."

"Looks aren't everything."

"No, but they don't hurt."

As shallow as that sounded, it was the way Trevor had chosen to deal with his own breakup, not his true heart, so Harrison let it pass. "I need to tell you something, and I want you to let me know if you think I'm off base or missing something."

"Sure. I'm listening." Trevor's tone turned serious, back to his old self.

Harrison drew a deep breath as if the air would blow courage into his heart. "It's probably nothing. But I've been thinking about my life and how things have changed so slowly for the past seventeen years that I didn't recognize it."

"You talking about Lisa?"

"Yeah. I thought I was in love with her when we got married, and maybe I was. But the infertility—it stole something from us. You remember how everything changed when she got that diagnosis, and she became more and more introverted."

"Yeah. I knew something had changed when she didn't want to have small group gatherings in your home anymore or get together with the rest of us."

"She couldn't handle it after you and Megan and the rest of our friends started getting pregnant and having children. It was hard for her to be the only one without them." Harrison picked up his drink again and traced a design in the moisture on the glass while lightning flashed outside his window. "Eventually, our lives shrank until there was nothing left but the childlessness."

Trevor hesitated. "I never knew for sure whether that was Lisa's fault."

"Both of us were at fault. I could have changed the tone of our relationship. But I didn't know how. It seemed like our marriage needed something neither of us knew how to give," Harrison said, realizing for the first time how wounded he'd been. "I wasted the past five years, and I'm finished doing that. I'm thinking about asking Anise out."

"For…a date?" Trevor's voice sounded tight, as if he were choking.

There was that word again. It had been terrifying enough when he'd admitted to himself that he wanted to ask Anise out. Hearing it out loud was even worse.

"Right. But I don't know where to take her," he said in an unfamiliar voice that sounded a little like a sixth-grader's. A deep-voiced little boy's.

Trevor lifted his mug from the side table, took a long gulp. Probably to recover from the shock. "Okay, what kind of things does she like?"

"That's the hard part. Anise doesn't have a lot of hobbies or indulgences. Her family and her church are the most important things in her life." He smiled, thinking of her devotion to those important things. "She's a great cook and she likes music and Christian romance novels. Anise is not the kind of woman you can impress with an expensive meal or a movie. I need a better idea."

"Not sure I'm the best guy to advise another man about romance…"

Harrison shook his head. "We both know you weren't to blame for Megan's problems or her death. You were the best husband you could be to her. And Jennifer—I'm glad you found out her true character before the wedding, not after. It doesn't mean you're not a great catch."

Trevor snorted. "Okay, then here's some advice from the man who failed epically in romance not once but twice—find out something she's always wanted to do but hasn't or couldn't."

Harrison thought about that, and then it hit him, and his nerves calmed a little. "What if it's something she can't do but wants to learn?"

That slow smile of Trevor's showed Harrison he was on the right track. "What is it? An art class? Flower arranging class? Oh, I know— find a place where you can learn how to make those fancy chocolates. You should do that."

"Nope. I just bought a Bronco with manual transmission. I'm going to teach her to drive a stick shift."

Trevor's raised brows showed his disapproval. "Bad idea. That's not a date. At least, not if you don't take her somewhere afterward."

"Then I'm back to the same problem—where to take her."

"Right, and you can't exactly ask any of her family for ideas. Especially Jase." Trevor hesitated as if in thought, then he gave Harrison that borderline-wicked grin of his that always meant trouble. "You said Anise thinks your landlady is a matchmaker. Ask her where to take Anise."

"No! That would make the matchmaking problem even worse." But Trevor was right— Miss Eugenia would know of a place where Anise would like to go. And she'd sure be eager to tell him. He'd have to think about that.

"I want to know one thing." Trevor's voice

turned serious, his brow furrowed. "Do you think you could fall for Anise?"

Good ol' Get-to-the-Point Trevor. "I'm not sure. Maybe."

"Then be warned. You know how this goes. A man teaches a woman to drive a manual transmission, and by the time he's done, they either hate each other or fall in love."

That was the problem. Because for him, the first option wasn't a remote possibility.

Chapter Nine

~❧~

The time Harrison both dreaded and longed for had nearly come.

Late the next afternoon, the skies remained dreary and the wind strong from last night's storm, and it left puddles for the patients to step around in the church parking lot. As Anise and Harrison closed the clinic for the day, he mentally ran through his plan for the evening. She'd already told him she'd be home alone tonight. So after work, he'd grab a quick shower, shave and put on a decent, casual outfit and some cologne. Then, armed with the daisies he'd pick up from the florist on the way home and the chicken marsala he'd prepped this morning, he'd head over to Anise's house. With fear and trembling, he'd ask her for a date and hope the flowers and food would bribe her to say yes.

Miss Eugenia would probably say it was bad

manners to ask for a date tonight, instead of a week or at least days in advance. But working together all day, every day in such close quarters while waiting for date night seemed awkward.

He remembered the text message Miss Eugenia had sent in reply to his request for date ideas last night.

The flower farm is her favorite place in the world. Teach her to drive your fancy new vehicle, then have a candlelight supper at the picnic table. Eugenia Price Mabel Stratton.

He probably should have called Miss Eugenia or asked her in person instead of texting, which to him was the lowest form of communication. But something inside him didn't want to see the victory that would surely shine in those aging hazel eyes if he went to her house for advice. Neither did he want to hear it in her voice if he called. Because Harrison knew that asking Anise out could go either way.

Miss Eugenia could do her celebrating after Anise said yes.

If she said yes.

But for now, Anise had her phone out, reading a text message of her own. "It's Miss Willa Mae," she said. "Listen to this—'Come quick.

Chantelle's baby is almost here. The daddy went to Memphis, and I got nobody to take us to the hospital.'"

That sounded bad.

"Poor Chantelle—and Miss Willa Mae," Anise said, her big brown eyes pooling with emotion. "I'll call and find out the situation. The Hatcher family doesn't need a dramatic home birth on top of all their other problems."

"If they need us, we'll have to get there quick." Harrison closed and locked the chair closet door while mentally reviewing labor and delivery procedures. "We might have to deliver that baby."

"I'll call her before we head out." She hit the dial button on the text message and turned on the speaker.

The phone rang only once before Miss Willa Mae answered. "Are you on your way?"

"We're almost ready to pull out of the church parking lot. But Chantelle needs to go to the hospital. Don't you have anyone else to take you besides the baby's daddy?"

"You know I ain't got no neighbors out here, except for old Miss Adah Corbin, and she hasn't had a car since 1999. I've called some friends but didn't get ahold of them. I can't spend time on the phone. Chantelle needs me."

Adah Corbin—Harrison remembered that farm a mile or so from the highway.

Anise muted the phone. "According to our policy, we can't transport patients, but we need to stop and check on her. And you're right—we might end up delivering the baby." At Harrison's nod, she unmuted. "We'll come, but you need to call an ambulance."

"Ain't got no time for an ambulance. Closest one is a half hour out, but you're only five minutes away. That baby's coming!"

"Call 911 anyway."

Anise hung up and turned to Harrison. "Do you have labor and delivery experience?"

"A little, but only when we were transporting trauma patients. An OB nurse always came along and took charge of the labor while I stabilized the mother's vitals." He opened a supply cabinet door and pulled out the emergency backpack. "But we can do it. While you finish shutting the place down, I'll gather delivery supplies and pray the baby isn't breach."

Within minutes, they headed to the cockpit, Harrison carrying the backpack. He took his phone from his pocket and pulled up an obstetrics website. "It wouldn't hurt to review treatment of labor and delivery complications. In the helicopter, I'm usually focused on keeping people alive, not delivering babies."

As they headed toward Mockingbird Creek, Harrison read procedures and complications to Anise, and they discussed possible scenarios and treatments. When they got to the turnoff to the Hatchers' home, the creek rushed by beside the road, swollen from last night's storm, its banks muddy and soggy-looking as the surrounding trees swayed in the wind.

Approaching the hairpin curve just before Miss Adah Corbin's farm, Anise fell silent, her focus on the narrow, wooded road.

Anise took the bend just as Miss Adah's donkey trotted out of the woods and into the middle of the road ahead of them.

"Bogey—" She hit the brakes, swerved to miss the animal.

The RV fishtailed and nose-dived toward the creek.

His left arm stretched out to Anise, Harrison braced himself with his right, and in a moment that felt like an hour, the RV crashed through the trees and down the embankment until it landed, nose first, in the water.

The RV had tipped at an odd angle, the cockpit several feet lower than the back, and branches partially obscured his view of the creek. He leaned forward and looked to the right, where the vehicle rested against the trunk of a giant tree.

After a stunned moment, he drew his hand away and turned to face her. "You okay?"

"I—think so. You?"

"Fine." He shifted his focus out the windshield and took in the sight of water cascading before them and a giant long-eared gray menace standing in the creek, staring back at him through the glass and braying. How had Bogey gotten down here so fast?

Then he realized they'd probably sat in silence after the crash longer than he'd thought.

"Bogey, you're a bigger troublemaker than your namesake." Anise slumped over the steering wheel, her elbow on the armrest and her chin in her hand, as she gazed out the windshield. She let out a huge sigh and looked up at Harrison with those beautiful eyes. "I guess we need to check out the damage."

Minutes later, after Harrison had put on the backpack and Anise had loaded her purse and tablet in her big tote bag, they stood on the creek bank and surveyed the wreck that used to be the mobile clinic.

"That big live oak tore up the side of the RV, and the creek bottom destroyed the front," Anise said, her voice shaking a little. She sank down in the mud in her high-heeled sandals, and Harrison held out his hand to steady her as they started up the bank. "I guess I shouldn't have swerved, but it was instinct. Although, even if I'd had time to think it through, I couldn't have intentionally hit Bogey. I've known him for at least fifteen years, when my boys used to come out here to play with Miss Adah Corbin's grandsons."

Of course she couldn't. But Harrison smiled at the idea of knowing a donkey.

Within minutes, they'd reached the road, the giant donkey nowhere in sight.

"We have two problems," Harrison said as they gazed down at the wreck. "Our clinic is stuck in a creek, and we have no way to get to our patient. Even if you could walk the four miles in those shoes, we'd probably get there too late. Are you sure the lady who owns Bogey doesn't have a car?"

"Positive."

"Who can we call to come and get us?"

"Do you have a phone signal? Because I can never get one out here."

He checked. "I can't either."

"We'll have to call from Miss Adah Corbin's house," Anise said, starting that way. "Harrison, the RV is in bad shape, isn't it?"

He drew a deep breath, wishing it wasn't so. "It's an old vehicle, and it has a lot of damage."

"As soon as we get back to town, I'll find a way to get it out of the creek and running again."

Running again? If Harrison knew anything

about vehicles, this one was ready for the scrapyard. But now wasn't the time to tell Anise. At this point, it looked as if the clinic had finished almost as soon as it had gotten started.

However, Anise would find a way to resurrect it. She wasn't one to give up, and she could do anything she set her mind to.

She kept her gaze down on the road, as if she knew she wasn't being realistic but didn't want to face the truth. "Maybe I made a mistake in driving out here. But Chantelle needs us, and she doesn't have anyone else to help."

Walking toward the Corbin farm, they brainstormed ways to go the four miles to Miss Willa Mae and Chantelle's house, but nothing came together.

When they reached the farm, Miss Adah Corbin didn't answer the door. "Someone must have picked her up," Anise said, jiggling the locked door handle.

"We have to think of a way to get there." Why was this so hard? Harrison had spent less time than this inventing spur-of-the-moment solutions during emergencies in a helicopter and had enough success to publish nursing journal articles about his innovations. So why couldn't he think of a way to get down a country road? "Let's look in her barn. Maybe there are some bicycles or something."

"On this muddy road, we couldn't get anywhere on a bike," she said.

That might be true, but they had to do something. "Let's look anyway."

As they started toward the barn, Bogey walked out and headed toward them as if he'd done nothing wrong. Harrison wouldn't have been surprised if the donkey was looking for Anise so she'd pet him.

Sure enough, the huge animal went right up to her and laid his head on her shoulder.

She set her tote on the ground.

"This is how we're getting to Chantelle," she said, standing at Bogey's head. "A lot of people don't know you can train donkeys to be ridden. Lead with your knee and jump. Get on your stomach first and then swing your right leg up and over, like this."

Obviously, she was experienced in donkey riding because, before he knew it, Anise was sitting on Bogey's back. And she apparently wanted Harrison up there too. "Uh, I don't even ride horses, let alone a giant—"

"If you can fly in a helicopter, thousands of feet in the air, you can ride this donkey." She slid off the animal's back and looked at him as if she thought he was going to get on.

"His back is five feet off the ground, and his head is as high as mine. Look, this King Kong of the donkey world has already destroyed a forty-foot RV. What makes you think I'd get off him alive?"

Her tinkling laugh merely added another measure of panic to his heart. "He's more like four and a half feet tall."

"You don't understand. I know nothing about riding a horse, let alone a monster like Bogey. His name should be Behemoth instead."

An encouraging smile replaced her soft laughter.

"Besides, this is not our donkey. You don't just walk up to somebody else's donkey, get on and ride it down the road." He wasn't about to ask how she'd learned to ride a mammoth donkey. "And even as big as he is, I don't think he can carry us both."

"I've known Miss Adah Corbin all my life, and she would never deny a donkey to someone in need. Especially when they need it to help her neighbor. There's a female in the barn. I'll ride her, and you can take Bogey."

As she strode into the barn, he called after her. "I'll bet her name is either Katherine or Hepburn."

"It's Bacall. Miss Adah Corbin loves *Key Largo* almost as much as she loves *The African Queen*."

Clearly, he was not getting out of this, but that didn't mean panic wasn't setting in. Even if he managed to get on the donkey's back, could he stay on? What would a live animal do once a man was up there?

Getting on Bogey's back would be less embarrassing if he did it before Anise returned. He stepped back and got a little start, then jumped.

The thing he got right was landing on the animal. The thing he got wrong was getting stuck lying crossways on its back. For some reason, he couldn't get his right leg around on the other side of the mammoth's body. So instead of straddling him with a dignified, manly, cowboy-like posture, Harrison merely flopped on his belly like a fish while the donkey twisted and pranced.

Bogey must have decided Harrison liked riding facedown and sideways, because the donkey took off at a fast clip.

"Wait a minute," he bellowed like a bull, hanging on to the donkey's mane with all his might. "Whoa, Bogey!"

Did donkeys even know the word *whoa*?

Apparently not. It took all Harrison's strength to keep from falling off. But the last thing he wanted was to be humiliated in front of Anise by letting her see him flounder around on his stomach on the back of a ridiculously huge donkey. Or by hitting the dust.

He tried another command. "Bogey, stop!"

This time, it worked. Before Anise rode Bacall out of the barn, Bogey had stopped and Harrison had somehow finally sat up and strad-dled the animal, having regained as much dig-nity as a man can have when he is sitting on a mile-high donkey.

"Let's get out of here," he said as Anise joined him. "How do you make a donkey go?"

"Tell him to walk." Anise stopped Bacall next to her tote bag, slid off and grabbed it, and then jumped back on.

Harrison never thought he'd say this to a woman, but… "Anise, you have great donkey-riding skills."

By the time they reached the house, Harri-son's backside was so sore, he vowed he'd never touch another donkey. But Miss Willa Mae had been right. Chantelle was about to deliver. And by the time the ambulance arrived, Anise had laid baby Everly in her mother's arms.

Miss Willa Mae had called the sheriff to de-liver the donkeys to their home and to pick up Harrison and Anise. When he dropped them off at the hospital, they headed for their office to record their day. While Anise posted pictures of the baby and the now-useless RV on social media, Harrison drew up all his courage and ap-proached her desk. Today they'd survived an ac-cident together, ridden donkeys to a home visit and delivered a baby.

Surely all those experiences had formed a closer bond between them.

It was time.

He rushed right in, afraid he'd chicken out otherwise. "I prepped some chicken marsala this morning. Would you like to come over and eat with me tonight? And then maybe we could drive out to your flower farm and look at the stars…"

She didn't look up from her computer monitor. "Thanks, but I might not make it home before midnight. I have to let my sponsors and donors and Jackson Memorial Hospital know what happened."

Harrison glanced at the screen. Sure enough, she was sending an email to Jackson Memorial. "I think it would be okay to wait until morning. You need to eat and get some rest tonight. It's been a long, hard day."

Anise finally looked at him and gave him a little smile. "That's very sweet. But if I learned anything tonight, it's that this clinic is absolutely vital in rural Adams County. So I have to hurry and raise the funds to get the RV fixed. What would have happened if we hadn't been there to deliver baby Everly?"

"Anise, none of that has to be done tonight."

"But this is my responsibility—"

"Then let me help. I have writing experience, so let me put together a fundraising letter."

"Thank you, but I have to do it myself."

She went back to her work. Harrison grabbed his keys from his desk and walked out. And when he turned the key in his Bronco and headed home, he was certain she hadn't even noticed he'd left.

Before dawn the next morning, Harrison dropped a pod into his coffee maker, feeling as if he'd ridden Bogey all the way back to San Diego rather than the short distance from Miss Adah Corbin's farm to Miss Willa Mae's. And his heart felt as bruised as his backside. Apparently, he was about as skilled in getting a date as he was in riding a donkey, since his first attempt in years had failed epically, abysmally.

His timing had been wrong. And maybe he'd been off the dating market so long, he didn't remember how to ask for a date. The more he thought about it, the worse it seemed.

When his coffee was done, he spooned in some sugar and sat at the table, gazing across the lawn at Anise's house. Her lights were off, which probably meant she was still asleep.

At least one of them could sleep.

He picked up his phone from the table, pulled up the text Anise sent last night, and read it for about the fifteenth time.

Please drop by the hospital in the morning and talk to Tara. I've asked her to reassign you to the ER for now. That way, you can keep working until I get the clinic on the road again.

Sure, he'd talk to Tara today so she could decide his future. But that didn't mean he wouldn't also go to Anise's office and try again to help her.

He skipped breakfast and got out his Bible and notebook for his morning study. An hour later, Anise's lights still hadn't come on, so Harrison changed into brown pants and a burgundy pullover and reached for his keys. When he let Tiny Romeo out, the little dog crawled through his hole and into Anise's yard as usual.

Sugar greeted him with a rumble in her throat and a sniff to his nose.

But what was she doing outside? Anise never let her dog out until she went to work.

Harrison opened the gate and strode across her lawn and up to her porch. He knocked quietly, in case she was sleeping. When she didn't answer, he decided to look in her garage window for her vehicles.

The scooter was gone. Either she left while he was getting dressed, or she went to work before he got up.

He had a feeling he knew which had happened.

Fifteen minutes later, he strode into the clinic office, the ER schedule in his hand with available shifts marked in red. He found Anise on the phone, focused on the notes she was taking in her planner.

With nothing else to do but check his work email, he sat at his desk and waited for her to end the call. But after five minutes, things started to feel awkward. He'd almost decided to leave when she hung up.

"Harrison." She said his name in her tender voice, as if she was glad to see him. "Tara told me she has room for you on the ER schedule. I was glad."

She was? Well, he wasn't. He wanted to be here, helping her get the clinic running again. In fact, he wanted to be wherever Anise was.

"I know my position here is considered closed. But I was hoping to give you a hand." He moved closer and pulled his old chair up to her desk. "Truth is, I'm not too interested in the ER. I'd rather help you get the RV fixed, or maybe find another one. Clearly, there's not pay available until the clinic's back on the road. But I'll volunteer my time. I have enough saved to support myself until we—"

"That's sweet of you," she said, glancing at her planner again, "but I'm doing fine."

What? He thought she'd be happy to have help. "If we work together, we'll get the job done faster."

Her phone rang, and she checked the number. "I can manage. But I have to take this. It's the wrecker."

"Anise, you can't manage. You came to work before five this morning, didn't you?"

She just smiled that sweet smile of hers and took the call.

Harrison stepped out and shut the door.

What had just happened?

He started for the parking garage, the schedule still in his hand.

If the phone hadn't rung, or if she hadn't answered, he might have convinced her to let him help.

And tried again for a date.

As it was, he had a whole day on his hands with nothing to do.

His stomach grumbled, and he considered stopping somewhere and getting a late breakfast, although nothing sounded good. Except maybe a couple of Jase's cinnamon rolls.

The thought of the rolls with their thick frosting jogged a memory he couldn't quite nail down. But it seemed he'd forgotten something that had to do with those rolls…

Then he remembered. It wasn't about the cinnamon rolls. It was a conversation he'd had with Jase while eating them.

I promise you, if things ever change and I want a romantic relationship with your mom, I will come and tell you myself. Even before I tell her. And if you want me to back off, I will.

He pulled over and dialed Jase.

"I heard about the RV," his son said. "Is it a total loss?"

"Probably, considering its age and damage."

"So you're out of a job."

"For now." He hesitated. "Do you have time to talk with me today?"

"Hang on. Let me check with Erin." Then, after a few moments of silence, "We're having a late breakfast. Want to join us?"

Harrison hadn't expected an invitation, and it warmed his heart. He quickly accepted and started for Rosewood.

Minutes later, he parked his bike in the drive behind the big house, went to the back door and let himself in as Jase had instructed him.

"We're in the kitchen," Jase called.

It felt strange to walk right into someone's home. Even he and Trevor didn't do that. They couldn't. They kept their doors locked in San Diego.

In the kitchen, Harrison found a place set for him between Jase and Miss Fannie.

"We heard what happened to the clinic," the older lady said as she picked up a platter of bacon and loaded a half dozen slices on his plate. "You need a good breakfast to help cheer you up. A little bacon will help."

"So will Jase's jumbo biscuits." Erin, sitting next to Bella's high chair, passed the biscuits and fried potatoes.

Later, as Harrison helped Jase clean the kitchen, he silently prayed for wisdom, since his new relationship with Jase could go either way after he heard what Harrison had to say.

"I have something on my mind, and I'm a little nervous about telling you." Actually, *terrified to tell you* would be a better description.

Jase didn't look up from the iron skillet he was cleaning. "Sounds like this has something to do with Mama."

While he knew the chances were good that Jase would have guessed the reason for his visit, his son's calm, almost matter-of-fact voice took Harrison aback. "Uh, yeah."

"I expected this, but not quite this soon. But go ahead and tell me."

His throat suddenly dry, Harrison set down his towel and took a sip from his water glass. Might as well put the truth out there all at once.

"You were right. I do have strong feelings for your mother. And I promised to tell you if things changed, so…"

This wouldn't have been half as awkward if things had gone differently—if Anise would have accepted his clumsy invitation.

"Have you told her?"

Harrison blew out a breath. "That was hard to do when she turned me down for a date."

"Oh."

The last thing Harrison expected was to hear the compassion Jase expressed in that single word, not to mention the softening in his eyes.

"Harrison, I'm sorry."

"What? I thought you'd be relieved."

"I'm never relieved when love goes wrong." Jase leaned against the counter and met Harrison's gaze. "You might not know that two women left me at the altar—literally—before I met Erin."

No, he hadn't. But the thought knifed his heart.

"I know what rejection feels like, so I would never rejoice in your pain. Or anyone else's." Jase's expression turned tender. "I see now that I made you feel rejected, and I'm sorry. I didn't see it at the time."

Even in the midst of his confusion about Anise's actions, Harrison couldn't help giving thanks for Jase and for the man he was. But he was smart enough to know that his son's compassionate, caring heart had come from Anise, not from him.

And he realized again what a special family he'd become a part of.

Thursday afternoon, Anise unlocked her office, half wishing she didn't need to put even one foot in there. She missed seeing patients, she missed her family and she missed Harrison.

She was tired of being alone.

Anise set down her purse and messenger bag, pulled out her planner and pen, and sunk into the office sofa. This week, she'd had enough of sitting at her desk, so she'd work here for at least a few minutes. Since her meeting with the mechanic hadn't gone any better than the first two, she had more work to do. She'd have the estimate on Monday, but it didn't sound as if this company's price would come in much lower than the others.

Her one bright spot this week was having Harrison stop by and bring her food every day. The gesture had boosted her spirits, not to mention that she probably wouldn't have taken time for a decent meal otherwise.

And offering to volunteer—she'd never forget his kindness.

But this was her responsibility. And honestly, she could work faster without someone else in the room.

She'd opened her planner and kicked off her favorite wedge sandals when a knock sounded at the door.

"Come in." She scrambled for her sandals and had one on when Harrison opened the door and strode in, carrying a Cupboard sack.

"Have you eaten?" A savory aroma wafted through the room. "Today's special is roast pork loin with muscadine sauce—whatever that is— rice, salad and broccoli corn bread."

"I love muscadines! They taste like Concord grapes."

He set the sack on her desk as she put on her other sandal.

For this, she could manage to sit at her desk. "I wouldn't have made it through this week without you, Harrison. Every day, you seemed to know just what I'd want to eat."

"I went for a run this morning and found a little Thai restaurant near to Commerce Street," he said, impossibly handsome in dark jeans and a blue button-down. "Can I take you there for dinner?"

She opened her sack and pulled out the pork loin. "That sounds nice, but I have a video call with Jackson Memorial late this afternoon, and

I have to spend the evening preparing for to-morrow, when I meet with my Natchez donors."

"Let me take the meeting. I'm working night shift this week, so tonight's my last shift until Monday. That gives me time to prepare and to meet with the donors."

That could work, since all eight sponsors loved Harrison, especially after they heard how he rode Bogey to help deliver the baby.

It would be nice to have some of her burden lifted. But what if something went wrong?

"Thank you, but I'd better do it myself."

At the disappointment in his eyes, she almost reconsidered.

"Then let me help you prepare for the meeting."

But Anise couldn't afford this kind of distraction, especially with the weekend coming. With her emergency meeting with Jackson Memorial's board at eight o'clock Friday evening and her meeting with Jackson area sponsors early Saturday morning, she'd have to spend the night. That meant she had to prepare for the meetings—and she had to be on her game—and pack for a night in a hotel. And take Sugar to Rosewood so Jase could take care of her. And a hundred other things, it seemed.

"Honestly, Harrison, I need time and space. I appreciate the offer, but there's a lot at stake."

"I want to help carry the load. Every day this week, I've come over to help. But you won't let me. You've shut me out."

How she wished she could let him help. But both her mother and Vernon taught her that nobody was ever really there in the way she needed them.

No hometown friends with hand-me-down clothes, no foreclosing banker with a charity shack, no generous friend with an offer to take care of her son could give Anise the help she needed.

The help she'd always wished for.

A partner.

Someone who wouldn't try to patch up her messes. But one who would take the load of aloneness from her and share responsibility, rather than expecting her always to be the only one with solutions. And even though Harrison wanted to help, Anise was the one who had driven the RV into the creek. That meant in the end, it was up to her to make this right.

She wished things were different, but people don't often get what they want, especially in relationships. "I'm sorry. I have to do this myself."

"Okay. I get it."

His words came out soft, a little sad, and for a moment, she thought he'd say something more.

But he just walked out the door.

Chapter Ten

Since nothing else was going right, Harrison might as well check Aero Trader's website for Dad's plane. Maybe the disappointment of not seeing the plane would distract him from the heartbreak of Anise shutting him out.

Not that this strategy would work. But if it could take his mind off Anise for a few minutes, it would be worth it.

In his den, Harrison settled into his favorite recliner, grabbed his tablet, pulled up Aero Trader and scrolled through the aircraft for sale. Then he spotted it—a light blue Skyhawk with shark jaws on its nose. Harrison would recognize that plane anywhere.

Scanning the details, he found that the registration number matched his dad's aircraft. And the price was reasonable…

Harrison shot an email to the owner then sat

back down and tried to let this change sink in—within days, he might finally fly his dad's plane.

About an hour later, the owner responded with maintenance records and an invitation to check out the aircraft.

Maybe he should go to San Diego and take a look.

Tomorrow, Trevor would fly himself home from visiting his daughter in Sacramento. Harrison could book a flight, arrive in the morning and check out the plane before Trevor got there in the afternoon. If Harrison decided to buy, he could rent the same hangar space the Skyhawk was in now, and Trevor wouldn't mind him staying at his house for a couple days. The Natchez airport manager had assured him of hangar space there, so Harrison could fly his dad's plane back to Natchez on Sunday.

Of course, he should think this through and pray about it. But the price was right, and Harrison could spare the money. And he'd been waiting years for the plane to go on the market, so it made sense to look at it.

He messaged Trevor, checked online and bought a ticket to San Diego. Then, realizing he should tell his son he was leaving, he texted Jase and asked him to stop by.

Before Harrison finished packing, the doorbell rang. He headed back downstairs and peered through the living room window.

Jase. Harrison opened the door.

"I was leaving Joseph's house when you texted," he said. "He's coming to church Sunday, so you'll meet him."

"I won't be here," Harrison said as they headed for the kitchen. He dropped a coffee pod into his machine and got out his favorite mug, the one that read #FlightNurseLife: An ER at 10,000 Feet. "I just booked a flight to San Diego to look at my dad's old plane. Maybe to buy it."

As Harrison handed him the coffee, Jase's eyes widened. "What? You're coming back, aren't you?"

"Unless you ask me not to." He could hardly believe the disappointment in Jase's face and tone.

"No, I want you to come back to stay."

He hesitated, his throat thick. "Then I will. No matter what."

"What about the clinic?" Jase asked. "You'll get it on the road again soon, won't you?"

Oh. Anise hadn't told him her repair difficulties. "Your mom's doing her best, but I doubt it."

"She's working way too much, trying to make it come together." Jase sipped his coffee, set it back on the counter. "Have you had that talk with Mama? You know, about your feelings?"

Harrison hesitated, his throat suddenly thick. "It didn't go so well."

"You told her?"

"I didn't get a chance. The night of the wreck, I did a lousy job of asking her out, so today I decided to be more straightforward. She turned me down flat."

"Did she say why?"

"She doesn't have time. I've been at her office every day this week to help her. But she has shut me out of her life."

Jase took a long drink of his coffee. "Is that the real reason you're going to San Diego?"

Was it? Maybe. Did he think Dad's plane would somehow heal the wounds Anise had re-opened? Wounds inflicted by his father's abandonment and his wife's disinterest? Not really.

"All I know is that she's made her feelings—or lack of feelings—clear."

Jase reached over and laid his hand on Harrison's shoulder. "I'm truly sorry, Harrison."

So was he. Because for the first time, he'd found a woman he would love to have been grounded with.

If Anise could go back and change the events of that fateful day and prevent the accident, she'd do it. Why did it have to fall apart—literally—just when everything was coming together? Jase had agreed to give Harrison a chance, Harrison was fitting into the family, and the clinic had been going great too. Until one renegade donkey's trek across the road ruined it all.

In her office at six on Friday morning, Anise still had much to do to get things back on track.

Harrison had been sweet about the clinic the night of the wreck, hoping to cheer her up with chicken. And with lunches too. It might have worked, if she hadn't had to keep pressing on to get the RV fixed.

Her phone buzzed with a text. She picked it up. Jase, asking if she was up. Surely he didn't think she would waste time sleeping in, with so much work to do.

She called him and hit speaker.

"What time are you going to work?" he asked.

Anise looked at her clock. She'd already been there an hour. "I'm at my office."

He hesitated. "I know what that clinic meant to you, but you can't spend all your time trying to resurrect it from the dead."

What was he thinking? It wasn't dead yet. "You don't understand all that's involved in getting it back on the road. For one thing, I have four bids for repairs, and they're all higher than our insurance will pay. If I can't find a mechanic and body man today, I have to find a new vehicle. I've been searching for one, just in case, along with writing a new support letter and meeting with my board and—"

"I get that, but we haven't seen you and have barely heard from you for the past week. You ignore your phone more than you answer it. Bella's been asking for you. Abe told me that Georgia thought maybe you went to heaven."

Her granddaughter's cuteness made her chuckle despite her frustration with her son.

"Mama, you don't understand. I was there, and it wasn't funny. Georgia was crying because one of the girls in her Sunday school class lost her grandmother last week, and Georgia was scared. She hadn't seen you or heard your voice for so long, she thought maybe you were…you know, gone too. With Jesus."

Oh. That was different.

Well, she didn't want Georgia to think that. She looked for an open spot in the planner sitting on her desk. "Okay, let's get together. How about Sunday right after church? I'll have about an hour before I have to—"

"No."

Her son's firm voice, interrupting her, startled her into silence.

"I know the clinic is important, but it's not the only thing in the world."

"I appreciate your concern. Everything will

get back to normal after the clinic is on the road again."

"Mama, I'm coming over there. Right now."

"No, you don't need to—"

Wait... *Call ended?*

Her son hung up on her?

More than a little irritated with Jase, Anise forced herself to ease back in her chair, to calm down, just now realizing how tense this conversation had made her.

Yes, she was working long hours, and she probably would for some time to come. Even though Jackson Memorial had promised to do what they could to continue to help support the clinic and fix the RV, they'd back out of their agreement if she didn't find someone to work on it soon. In that case, she'd need to find support elsewhere, since the small Natchez hospital didn't have the funds to help.

Five minutes later, Jase's distinctive knock sounded at the door.

"Mama?" He opened the door and stuck in his head. "I'm glad you're alone so we can talk."

Anise chose not to point out the fact that she was typically alone at six thirty in the morning.

"I have to meet with a bride and groom this morning, so I don't have much time. But I need to ask you a question." He rolled Harrison's chair over to her desk and sat down, gazing at her with compassion in his big blue eyes. "How long do you plan to keep working sixteen-hour days?"

She blew out a sigh. "I've worked hard all my life. Why call me on it now?"

Jase hesitated. "Couldn't Harrison help you?"

What was Jase thinking? "There was nothing for him to do. I have to be the one to research other options, make the calls and meet with Jackson Memorial Hospital and my donors and supporters."

"You had to do all that yourself? Work sixteen-hour days every day when Harrison was right there all along, wanting to help and having as much interest in the clinic as you had?"

Well, when he said it that way…

"Did you know he left town?"

A cold chill ran through her. He left without saying goodbye? "When? Where did he go?"

"Yesterday. To San Diego," he said.

Anise pushed back her chair, then stood and paced the room. "Why? When is he coming home?"

"He has something important to do there, and he said he didn't know how long it would take."

She strode back to her desk. "What did he go there to do?"

"It's not my place to divulge his personal

life. That conversation needs to be between you and him."

Jase said it with a tone of a deeper meaning, and she knew what he was getting at. "There is no 'me and him.' We're friends who work together and share a son."

"He doesn't think so. He asked you for a date."

She blinked, trying but failing to understand. "A date? When?"

"The evening of the wreck, when you two came back to the office. And again yesterday."

Anise could only stare at him, and after a moment, her gaze darted about the room, unsettled, her eyes stinging. She drew in a breath, swallowed hard.

She thought back to their conversation after the wreck.

I prepped some chicken marsala this morning...

Would you like to come over and eat with me tonight?

And then maybe we could drive out to your flower farm and look at the stars...

And then again yesterday. *I went for a run this morning and found a little Thai restaurant near to Commerce Street...*

Jase was right. Harrison had been asking her for a date, but she didn't pick up on it.

But if he'd wanted to date her, why had he left?

Left without telling her he was going.

Just like Vernon.

She swiped at the corners of her eyes and sniffed a little. Suddenly weak, she collapsed in her chair. "No," she whispered. "I didn't realize. Why did he talk to you about this?"

"Because you both had been so adamant about not dating. He thought he owed it to me to tell me when his feelings changed."

Knowing her son's ability to see beyond the surface, he probably knew hers had changed too.

"Harrison also said you refused to let him help get the clinic running again. He said he came by every day this week, trying to help, but you completely shut him out. I think you should call him and apologize." Jase stood and gave her a quick hug. "I have to go so I can be ready when the bridal couple gets to Rosewood."

Thinking back, she couldn't remember seeing or hearing Harrison's little dog yesterday. "Where is Tiny Romeo?"

"Miss Eugenia took him home with her after Harrison left."

When he'd gone, Anise stood and paced to the window to watch her son, the bright parking lot lights making him easy to spot in the still-dark early morning, looking just like his father in the artificial glare. Even his gait reminded her of Harrison.

Harrison...

Oh, she should have been more careful, should have guarded her heart as she always had since Vernon left them, betraying her and the boys.

She'd never let any man worm his way in. And plenty had tried. So why had she allowed Harrison to invade her life, make her laugh, make her feel special?

Make her fall in love with him.

How had she let herself get so caught up in the clinic that she'd missed his invitation for a date? Worse, how had she not even noticed he'd left town?

She wandered back to her desk and stood behind it, her attention returning to the chair her son had used—Harrison's chair. The memories and warmth of the two men's presence threatened to take her breath. Harrison gone. Jase still here, still loving her, still trying in his own way to help her through this heartbreaking time...

Then she caught a glimpse of the monitor, where she had her email pulled up.

The mechanic had responded with an estimate, and so had the bodywork man.

Her pulse bounding, Anise scrolled down to the bottom line and let her gaze hover over the number that crushed her dream as completely as the creek bottom had crushed the RV.

She clicked out of her email account and turned off the computer. With the lowest bid for mechanic work alone costing nearly triple the vehicle's value, the clinic was gone.

And Harrison had disappeared without a goodbye, just when she thought she might risk rejection again. Somehow, that seemed the worst circumstance, the most painful of all, even more than Vernon.

Anise picked up her phone, pulled up her recent calls, and gazed down at Harrison's number and his contact picture. All she had to do was hit the button, and he'd answer, and he'd tell her why he'd done it. Why he couldn't stick around and be here for her, for their son.

She stopped, her finger hovering over the phone.

How many times had she called Vernon to ask him to come home, to be there for his family, for her?

She knew exactly how many times. Ninety-three. Three times a day for a month. And she knew how many times he'd answered.

Zero.

She turned off the phone and dropped it into her purse. Leaving behind her tablet and planner, she walked out. Locked the door. Because the clinic was done.

Just as she and Harrison were done.

She'd been right all along. It was better to be alone.

Chapter Eleven

Usually, when Harrison landed at the San Diego International Airport, he watched for the comforting sight of palm trees as the plane dropped in altitude and approached the runway. But this time, arriving out of sorts and fighting a bad mood, he hadn't even looked for those palms.

He missed the live oak in his backyard. He missed Tiny Romeo and Jase and Sugar.

He missed Anise.

Now at the airport again, he had a check in his wallet, ready to complete the transaction if the mechanic's report and flight log checked out. He and Trevor, who pulled his suitcase behind him, approached the hangar where Dad's old plane waited.

"I can't wait to see the Skyhawk," Harrison said.

"Me too. I've wanted to see this plane for

years," Trevor said, sounding as excited as Harrison felt. "I never thought you'd see it again, let alone buy it."

Neither did Harrison.

They rounded the corner of the hangar, and he caught his first glimpse of the plane, sitting outside in the Southern California morning sunshine, its blue body spotless and gleaming in the sunlight, its shark jaws bold and beautiful. And in the space of a moment, he became that disappointed little boy again, learning his father had sold the plane and he wouldn't get his birthday flight.

Did old memories like these ever go away? Or did they continue to fester year after year until you finally got to Heaven, where the Father would wipe away your tears?

Today, it felt as if no one but the Lord could ease his pain or take away this sense that no matter what he did, he'd never be enough for the people he loved—Dad, Martin, Jase.

And Anise.

Oh, Anise...

It was time to admit that yes, he'd fallen in love with her. And what better place to do that than standing here, next to this plane?

Wouldn't you know he'd discover he loved Anise right after she'd shut him out, just as Dad had, just as Lisa had.

In grave danger of letting that mood set in again, he introduced himself and Trevor to the plane's current owner and explained his connection to it. "I've dreamed of owning this plane since I was twelve years old, when my dad sold it," he said.

"Then I hope you buy it and get lots of enjoyment out of it." The man gave the plane's nose an affectionate pat, almost as if it were a pet dog.

That thought made Harrison homesick for Tiny Romeo all over again.

They checked out the engine and cockpit, and Trevor's mechanic declared the plane sound. The flight log looked good too, so after a few test flights, with each man taking a turn at the controls, Harrison became the owner of his father's aircraft.

"I'm glad you made it home in time to check out the plane with me." As he and Trevor headed to the parking lot, he looked over his shoulder for a last glimpse. "Seems like forever since you and I flew together."

Trevor flashed him a grin. "That's because you fell in love since then. Love somehow changes our perception of time."

It sure did. "Thanks for letting me stay at your place this weekend."

He stared Harrison down. "What, no comeback? No adamant denial that you're in love with Anise?"

He puffed out a big breath. "Nope."

"No way." His friend came to a dead halt in the middle of the lot. "Wait—if you're in love with her, what are you doing here?"

"Unfortunately, it isn't mutual."

"I don't believe it. You're the best catch in Southern California." He grinned. "Other than me."

He hesitated, then told Trevor about the accident, leaving out the part about Bogey, and how Anise had stepped into her office and out of his life.

"I decided to ask her out. She didn't even look up from her computer. Just flat-out turned me down. I kept trying to help get the RV running again, but she said no." They reached the car, and Harrison got in the passenger side. "I know the clinic is important, but she shut me out. Completely."

"Dude, that's brutal. I'm sorry."

Yeah, so was he.

"But you found Jase and Bella, so the trip was a success anyway."

Trevor's voice sounded a little too bright, but it was nice of him to try.

"So you came home to buy the plane. What

are you doing next? Staying here or going back to live close to Jase?"

"Going back. Other than a couple changes of clothes and my shaving kit, everything I have is still in Natchez."

Including his heart.

He grimaced. What would he do with the plane, anyway? Just as before, he had no one to fly with. Except Trevor, and that wasn't the kind of companionship he wanted.

Lord, what's the plan? Where do I go from here? I feel kind of lost. I don't even know why I have that plane...

Then it hit him, and he knew exactly what to do. "Turn around. I'm flying back to Natchez tonight."

"Right now?" Trevor's voice had raised an octave.

"I need to get home."

Somehow, the thought of flying his father's plane didn't bring the joy, the sense of anticipation he'd always thought it would. Because at this point, Harrison would rather be grounded than live without Anise.

Harrison landed the Skyhawk at the Natchez-Adams County Airport the next afternoon, having stopped in Abilene to sleep. Stepping from the plane, he pulled out his phone to request a ride share and saw that he'd missed four calls from Jase in the past hour.

Something had to be wrong. His pulse bounded as he dialed his son's number.

Jase answered immediately.

"I'm sorry to bother you, especially since you can't do anything from California, but I needed to talk to you," Jase said, his voice deep and cracking. "Erin and the babies are in trouble."

Harrison's heart gave a lurch as every possible scenario raced through his mind. "What's happening?"

"Her face and hands were swollen this morning, and she had a bad headache. Her blood pressure was sky-high. They can't get it under control."

"Preeclampsia?"

"Yeah. They'd already planned to do a C-section, but not this early. Harrison, I'm... I'm scared."

To be honest, Harrison was leaning in that direction himself. "Is your mother with you?"

"I can't get ahold of her. She went to Mockingbird Creek to tell some of her patients that she was shutting down the clinic. You know how the cell signal is out there."

He sure did.

"I know the Lord is in control, but..." A little Piper took off, drowning out Jase's words.

"Where are you?" he asked when the roar died down. "What was that noise?"

"A plane taking off. I'm at the Natchez airport."

"What? You're in town?"

"I just got here." Harrison decided to leave it at that for now.

Jase hesitated. "Will you come to the hospital? Stay with me until the babies are born and everybody is okay?"

He thought his heart might explode right there at the airport. "I'm on my way."

Ten minutes after he'd explained the situation to the airport manager and caught a ride with the man's assistant, Harrison all but sprinted into the obstetrics waiting room, and Jase came in soon after.

"Things are moving along fast, so I have only a moment." He swiped his hand across his eyes, tension all over his face. "I wanted to see you. To know you were here."

"I'm here and I'm staying." Harrison's voice came out ragged, husky. "Nothing could drag me out of this waiting room until the babies are born."

He hesitated, then tentatively, carefully, he gave Jase a quick hug and released him.

His son stood as if stunned, staring at him, eyes wide, not responding.

Okay, apparently the hug was a bad idea...

All of a sudden, Jase launched at him and wrapped him in the tightest, strongest embrace Harrison ever had. And as he held his son, he couldn't help speaking the words that filled his mind, his heart—his world. "Jase, I love you, son. You're a good man and a great dad, and I'm proud of you."

Determined to hold him as long as Jase wanted, Harrison just stood there, loving his son, quietly speaking words of blessing, of commitment, in a deep, raspy voice he'd never before heard falling from his mouth. And when Jase finally pulled away, his eyes wet and his nose a little runny, Harrison had to wipe his eyes too.

"My adoptive dad never hugged me. Never said he was proud of me or loved me." Jase hesitated. "Never called me son."

Harrison had to swallow back the lump that threatened to choke him, amazed how much Vernon missed out on.

Jase looked at his watch. "I have to get back in there... Dad."

His jaw working to hold back his emotions at hearing that special word spoken to him, Harrison reached in his pants pocket, pulled out a handkerchief and gave it to Jase. "Go."

Jase grinned at him and headed back to the

labor room while Harrison embedded the moment in his memory.

The moment he'd become a real father.

Hours later, on the faux-leather sofa in Erin's hospital room, Harrison gazed down at Oliver and Mia, one tiny baby in each arm.

Jase lounged on the bed with Erin across the room and snapped a picture at the exact moment Anise walked in.

Even the babies couldn't take Harrison's focus from her.

Sweet, anxious, beautiful—confused—she stood in the doorway, taking his breath as her gaze landed on him, lingered there for a moment.

"Harrison..."

Her whisper of his name made him want to leap off the sofa and pull her into his arms, never let go.

But his arms were full of his new grandchildren. And besides, she didn't want him.

She took a tentative step toward Harrison, then stopped.

He glanced around the room. The only other seat was a straight-backed wooden chair. "There's room for you here on the sofa."

When she'd reached him, he shifted a little, figuring she'd take one of the babies and then move far away from him to the hard chair. But instead, she sat beside him and gazed at Oliver, the baby nearest her.

"He looks like you," she said, brushing her hand over Oliver's head. "He has your eyes."

"He does?"

She nodded, smiling at the alert baby with that soft look he'd seen so many times. When her attention returned to Harrison, she seemed to pull back, to distance herself from him.

It didn't feel right.

The birth of twin babies should be a happy, drama-free event. But at this point, nothing in his life exuded peace right now, except his budding relationship with Jase.

Lord, why can't I be enough for her?

He should be content to have a son and three grandchildren. But something inside him would never feel complete without Anise—her gentle voice, her love for her family, her smile that could take his breath away.

"May I hold him, Harrison?"

Her humility went straight to his heart. Harrison was the newcomer, not her. He should ask her permission, not the other way around. "Sure."

As much as he hated to admit it, something felt right about her sitting next to him, sharing a moment, holding their grandchildren. Anise was so kind, so giving, it might work for them to live in the same town and share a family. But only if Harrison could keep an emotional distance from her, steel himself against her.

That's what he'd do.

Because at this moment, he realized being grounded sometimes meant you got to put down roots. And he wanted those roots, to be part of a family, have people to care about and take care of, to be there for them and share a life with them.

Yes. For the rest of his life, Harrison would be here with his son, his daughter-in-law and his grandchildren.

Grounded. And grateful for it.

For the first time since she decided to start a mobile clinic, Anise slept in.

And why not? She didn't have a job to go to.

She glanced at her bedside clock. Seven thirty. After more than eight hours of sleep, she still didn't feel rested.

The lack of purpose probably did that to people.

A sharp rapping at the front door made her heart pound for a moment. Harrison?

Then her good sense returned. Of course it wasn't Harrison. He had no reason to be here. Besides, he used the back door. And he would have Tiny Romeo with him, so Sugar would raise a fuss. Although Anise had no idea how her dog always knew whether or not Tiny Romeo was there before she could see or hear him. Or maybe even smell him.

Anise leaned over and peered under the high bed. Sure enough, Sugar was still lying there, conked out on the rug, directly below Anise. The same place the dog always slept when it thundered, as it had last night.

Surely nothing had gone wrong with Erin or the babies...

She got up and slung her pink waffle robe over the joggers and T-shirt she'd worn to bed and headed, barefoot, down the stairs. In the living room, she pulled back her curtain and caught sight of a sunflower-and mum-bedecked golf cart in her driveway.

What would Miss Eugenia be doing here at this hour?

Anise would soon find out because there she stood on the front gallery, a coffee cake and a jar of kimchi in her hands.

What a combination first thing in the morning.

Anise opened the door wide, and Miss Eugenia trotted in, clearly on a mission of some sort.

"I had a feeling Erin was going into labor soon, so I made a batch of kimchi," she said, heading for Anise's kitchen. "I dropped off a jar at Rosewood on the way here. It'll help Erin recover from the anesthesia."

That was a new one to Anise. She followed Miss Eugenia through the butler's pantry to the kitchen, where the older lady stuck the jar into the refrigerator.

Then she turned and sat at the kitchen table. "It took you longer than usual to answer the door. Were you still in bed?"

Brushing a lock of unruly hair from her eyes and pulling her robe tighter around her, Anise wasn't sure whether that was a rhetorical question. "I didn't need to be anywhere today, other than to see the babies. So I slept in."

"Well, it wasn't like you didn't have an opportunity to work. The ER, Dr. Slater's office… what was the other one? A clinic?"

How had she known about the offers Anise had yesterday? "The ortho clinic."

"Oh, yes. Dr. Hansford, the bone doctor, wanted you so much that he was willing to let you set your own hours and take Fridays off."

Anise resisted the urge to roll her eyes. She'd been right. Miss Eugenia's spy network had spread all over Natchez. "I haven't made a decision."

"Harrison's thinking about applying in Jackson as a flight nurse. He'll work twelve-hour shifts, but the hospital has a small apartment building for out-of-town employees. He'll stay there when he works two or more days in a row."

So Miss Eugenia had been talking to Harrison. Reporting his business was apparently her main purpose for coming over this morning. And she'd used her famous kimchi as an excuse to fix them up.

The little matchmaker had missed her mark this time, for sure.

"Harrison is in love with you, you know," Miss Eugenia said as if she were merely informing Anise of his favorite food.

Little did she know about Harrison's true feelings. "He left, Miss Eugenia. Without saying goodbye or telling me why. That's not what love does."

"Love doesn't push people away just because they're going through a hard time either."

Anise's face flamed. "Have you been talking to Jase?"

"Jase isn't pushing Harrison away anymore. That's why Harrison was at the hospital when Erin had the babies. Jase called him and asked him to come. Love is all about sticking together through hard times."

Yes, her son had told her that. At least, the part about having called Harrison.

"But Harrison left—"

"Because you pushed him away. Love draws near. 'Draw nigh to God, and He will draw nigh to you.' God's not the only one who does that. People do too." Miss Eugenia stood and grabbed a bread knife from the knife block. Then she cut a thick slice of coffee cake and set it in front of Anise. "Thanks to social media, Natchez loves Harrison as much as it loves you. Especially since the story leaked about you two riding donkeys to deliver a baby. That's big news around here. If you'd allowed Harrison to help, the two of you together would have that clinic back on the road by now."

Probably. Anise took a bite of the breakfast treat. Wow, it was even better than Miss Eugenia's usual baking.

"Harrison has something to tell you. I advise you to let him in and listen." She headed for the front door so fast Anise had to rush to catch up, her slice of coffee cake still in her hand. "Don't dillydally around. Hurry and get dressed. He'll be here any minute."

And he probably had kimchi in his refrigerator and a coffee cake on his counter.

It looked as if Miss Eugenia had started spying out people's personal schedules now too. Which didn't surprise Anise a bit.

Regardless, she took the older lady's advice and dashed up the stairs to shower.

Twenty minutes later, she dressed in her new wide-leg jeans, which reminded her of pictures of her mom in her bellbottoms, and a flowy white top. Then she pushed a bobby pin into her messy bun and ran downstairs, barefoot with her new bright orange autumn pedicure.

She'd just dropped a coffee pod into her coffee maker when she heard Sugar's toenails on the wooden stair treads. Within moments, Tiny Romeo's crying sounded from the back gallery.

Then a knock on the door.

She looked through the window. Harrison.

The sight of him drew the same sense of loss she'd struggled with yesterday in Erin's hospital room. Could she have been wrong about Harrison's leaving?

Before opening the door, she had to seek the face of the Lord.

Please, don't let me make a mistake. I'm afraid to draw near to Harrison...

When she opened the door and he walked into the room, hesitation filled those gorgeous blue eyes. She had a sense that he was about as likely to turn and walk back out as he was to stay and tell her whatever news Miss Eugenia said he had.

"My father's airplane went up for sale in San Diego this week, and I bought it." His words came fast, as if he wanted to spit them out and then leave. "If you'll set up a charity auction and use the proceeds to buy another vehicle for the clinic, I'll donate the plane. It should get you enough for a substantial down payment, and maybe other donations would cover the rest."

Substantial? It would probably pay for at least three quarters of the clinic cost.

More important, he was here. And he'd bought his father's plane... "Harrison, I don't know what to say. That's so generous, and I feel terrible about how I've treated you. I didn't mean to hurt you."

A fraction of the tension left his eyes. "I wanted to help. Still do. I've been thinking about something else," he said. "You never got your driving lesson."

She couldn't stop the grin that wanted to bloom on her face. "My stick shift lesson?"

"How about tonight? We can stay at the hospital until this afternoon. Then we'll go to Mockingbird Creek, on a back road where there's hardly any traffic, and I'll teach you to drive a manual transmission. Would you like that?"

Anise closed her eyes for the briefest moment and breathed a prayer of thanks. Because she'd only ever dreamed of a man looking at her the way Harrison was looking at her now. As if she were special. As if he would stay.

"Yes, Harrison. I'd like to."

When he started for the door, she had a feeling he'd come back often, maybe forever. And she'd never dreamed forever would feel this good.

Harrison had never seen a prettier sight than Anise in the driver's seat of his Bronco.

He'd removed the top and all four doors, and now as they cruised down Mockingbird Creek Road, her hair tumbled from its topknot, blowing in the warm autumn breeze.

It flowed around her face, long and wavy, just as it had the first time he'd seen her, on her back porch as he searched for Tiny Romeo. It was a good thing Harrison wasn't driving, because he couldn't have kept his eyes on the road.

"I think I'm getting the hang of it." Anise's rich brown eyes shone in the rays of the setting sun as she downshifted and rounded the last bend in the road before the flower farm.

"You're doing great." He pointed toward Anise's property as they approached it. "Let's take a break."

Anise pulled in the weedy driveway and turned off the engine. "The last time I felt a sense of accomplishment this strong was when I received my GED."

"Not nursing school or NP school?"

She shook her head. "I didn't think I could get

my GED, partly because I had no confidence and partly because I was raising my sons alone. But once I had it, I knew I could graduate from nursing school and get my master's degree."

Maybe Anise had once been timid enough to doubt her abilities, but right now, Harrison was the nervous one. They'd gotten through the driving instruction without hating each other. He could only hope Trevor had been right about the rest, because he had something to say to Anise. Something that would change their lives, regardless of her reaction. It was risky, and Harrison knew it. But it had grown too big, too overwhelming, to ignore.

They ambled to the picnic tables, then Harrison reached in his pocket for the key Jase had given him. He unlocked the little potting shed the family now used as storage, then he reached in for his thermos of coq au vin, basket of plates and silverware and candles, and a cooler with sparkling raspberry water.

"A picnic in my favorite place." Anise's eyes shone as if he'd taken her to San Diego's most exclusive restaurant.

"To celebrate your latest accomplishment."

After they'd set out the food and lit the candles and Harrison had said grace, Anise took a long sip of her raspberry water and then worked her fingers through her hair. "I need to get this mess under control before we eat. It's going to be tricky, since my hair elastic broke."

She pulled a couple of bobby pins from the strands and then started to pull back her hair.

He reached across the table and took her hand. "It's not a mess. It's beautiful."

"It's unruly."

"No, it's wavy and soft-looking and beautiful. I wish you'd wear it down more often."

He'd never forget her stunned expression as she lowered her hands and dropped the pins on the table.

Harrison got up, rounded the table, and stood next to her, looking into those brown eyes. "Anise, I need to tell you something. This has happened way faster than I ever thought it could, but everything is falling into place and all the pieces fit together—"

At her confused expression, he stopped. He was bungling this, big-time. And no wonder. He was in over his head, falling in love with a woman like Anise. "I'm talking about you and me, and Jase and me, Bella—even Miss Eugenia."

She still wasn't getting it. Her tilted head and concerned eyes told him so.

He let out a big breath and prepared himself for the crash of his life. "Anise, I'm trying to tell you that I love you."

He lowered his gaze, unable to watch as she shredded his heart. He waited, silent, for the blow.

Then she did the last thing he'd have expected her to do—she bounded to her feet and let out her beautiful, tinkling laugh.

Her arms wrapped around his waist. "Harrison, I've loved you since I watched you leap over my fence."

She had? She loved him?

He surprised himself by laughing too and realized for the first time how joyful true love is.

Anise drew closer and lifted her face to his, her eyes slipping closed.

But no. No way was he going to let her kiss him first this time. He took her in his arms and kissed her, twining a lock of her hair around his hand.

She tasted of raspberries and her hair smelled of flowers and sunshine, and as she kissed him back, the years of insecurities and disappointment faded away, a sense of permanence and contentment taking root in their place.

"Let's not waste any time. I want to be a real family with you and Jase and Abe and all the children as soon as we can."

She smiled. "You know I'm going to make you sing me to sleep every night."

As long as she was there, he was good with that.

And when he kissed her again, his old pain seemed to ease, leaving behind a residue of peace. How could love bring a gift like that? He'd never dreamed he'd find both a son and the love of his life as he embraced his past.

Epilogue

While Harrison wasn't nervous about his wedding, his insides knotted as he waited for Anise to see his wedding present to her. It was risky, but ever since the idea slammed into his brain the night of her driving lesson, he knew he had to try.

With the clinic benefit auction over and a new van purchased, they had a whole week to honeymoon before rolling out the clinic again. And Harrison wanted to start it right, with what he hoped would be a great memory for Anise.

Now, on this warm October Saturday, Harrison and Trevor turned in at Mamaw Vestal's Flower Farm and pulled into the newly rocked driveway.

Jase must have heard the crunch of tires on gravel—a new sound here—because he came running from the house before they made it out of the Bronco.

"Did you pull it off?" Harrison asked, hearing the stress in his own voice as he flicked a bit of dust from his new black suit jacket.

"She didn't open her eyes until I got her inside the house."

Good. The surprise was in place. Now all he had to do was to pray that she liked it.

Before long, their guests began to arrive, and Harrison, Jase and Trevor greeted each family. When it seemed all their guests had taken a seat before the makeshift outdoor altar, Jase signaled Harrison that it was time to start.

He took one last look around the farm and, seeing everything in place, he went to the house that had been Anise's grandmother's, stepped onto the porch and knocked on the door.

Anise answered his summons, wearing a soft blue dress that flowed around her ankles, her hair down and beautiful, and carrying a simple bouquet of white daisies. Zeke, leading a string trio, coaxed the beginning notes of "Canon in D" from his cello.

Harrison held out his arm, and she slipped her hand in the crook of his elbow, her sweet smile warming and reassuring him as always.

From the porch, she first looked toward the manicured lawn, then the weedless rows of mums and asters in the fields and the fresh paint on her grandmother's house and wooden fences.

"Harrison, what did you do?" she whispered as her calm, ladylike smile exploded into an expression of joy. "It looks as beautiful as it did when Mamaw was alive."

"I wanted our wedding to erase the bad days of your past while preserving the good ones. That way, we can build a new, better future for us and our family."

He kept his focus on her as she looked the other way, toward the old bait and liquor store, and he knew the moment the truth registered in her mind.

The store was gone, replaced with freshly sown grass, a few mums transplanted from the fields, and a flower-covered trellis.

Anise's hand shot to her mouth, her eyes wide and damp. And right there, in front of fifty wedding guests seated in rows of white wooden chairs, just outside prim and proper Natchez, she threw her arms around him, her bouquet forgotten as it dropped to the ground.

"Do you like your wedding present?" he asked.

"Harrison," she said in that way she had—the one that always sounded like whispered love streaming from within her. "I can't imagine anything better."

He retrieved her flowers, and they walked the too-long distance to the arch, where Jase waited, his black Bible open.

"Dearly beloved," Jase's deep voice rang out as he recited from memory, "we are gathered here today in the sight of God…"

Hours later, with the wedding meal a memory and the last guest gone, they headed for the airport. When they'd parked the Bronco and retrieved their luggage, Harrison started for the terminal.

Anise stopped him, her hand on his arm. "I have a wedding present for you too."

Bypassing the terminal, she led him to the hangars instead. He caught sight of the Skyhawk, sitting outside and looking beautiful in the sun's late-afternoon rays.

"Harrison, you're not sitting back and riding to Ocean Springs. You're flying us."

What? "How? We auctioned it off."

"The man who bought your father's plane is on my clinic board. I asked him to let us use it this week."

He was—flying them?

She cupped his face in her hands. "Harrison, as long as I live, you will always have someone to fly with."

As they boarded the Skyhawk, he realized he could get another plane, and he could get another job. But another flight partner? No, there would never be anyone but Anise, laughing at his corny jokes, making him feel secure, balancing his drive with her intuitiveness. Filling his heart, his future, his world.

Grounding him.

Because being grounded wasn't so bad after all.

* * * * *

If you enjoyed this emotional romance, don't miss Christina Miller's other stories featuring the Armstrong family:

Finding His Family
An Orphan's Hope

Available now from Love Inspired.

Find more great reads at
www.LoveInspired.com.

Dear Reader,

Thank you for joining me and the Armstrong family in my beloved Natchez! I've looked forward to telling Anise's story and seeing Jase learn to love his birth father.

I also loved sharing the "romance" between the real-life Sugar and Tiny Romeo. As in the story, we shared Tiny Romeo with his country neighbor owners a half-mile away. The two dogs were inseparable.

James 4:8 gives us a beautiful Bible promise: if we draw near to God, he will draw near to us. When Anise couldn't solve her problems, she drew near to God, and she wasn't disappointed. I've followed Jesus for thirty-seven years, and I can tell you he always shows up.

I would love to hear how Jesus has shown up for you! Contact me through Love Inspired, Facebook (@christinalinstrotmiller) and Twitter (@CLMillerbooks). Check out Sugar and Tiny Romeo on Facebook (@SugarDogMiller).

Christina Miller

COUNTRY LEGACY COLLECTION

19 FREE BOOKS IN ALL!

Cowboys, adventure and romance await you in this new collection! Enjoy superb reading all year long with books by bestselling authors like **Diana Palmer, Sasha Summers and Marie Ferrarella!**

YES! Please send me the **Country Legacy Collection!** This collection begins with 3 FREE books and 2 FREE gifts in the first shipment. Along with my 3 free books, I'll also get 3 more books from the **Country Legacy Collection**, which I may either return and owe nothing or keep for the low price of $24.60 U.S./$28.12 CDN each plus $2.99 U.S./$7.49 CDN for shipping and handling per shipment*. If I decide to continue, about once a month for 8 months, I will get 6 or 7 more books but will only pay for 4. That means 2 or 3 books in every shipment will be FREE! If I decide to keep the entire collection, I'll have paid for only 32 books because 19 are FREE! I understand that accepting the 3 free books and gifts places me under no obligation to buy anything. I can always return a shipment and cancel at any time. My free books and gifts are mine to keep no matter what I decide.

☐ 275 HCK 1939   ☐ 475 HCK 1939

Name (please print)

Address   Apt. #

City   State/Province   Zip/Postal Code

Mail to the Harlequin Reader Service:
IN U.S.A.: P.O. Box 1341, Buffalo, NY 14240-8571
IN CANADA: P.O. Box 603, Fort Erie, Ontario L2A 5X3

Visit
ReaderService.com
Today!

As a valued member of the Harlequin Reader Service, you'll find these benefits and more at ReaderService.com:

- Try 2 free books from any series
- Access risk-free special offers
- View your account history & manage payments
- Browse the latest Bonus Bucks catalog

Don't miss out!

If you want to stay up-to-date on the latest at the Harlequin Reader Service and enjoy more content, make sure you've signed up for our monthly News & Notes email newsletter. Sign up online at ReaderService.com or by calling Customer Service at 1-800-873-8635.